Endless Love

First printing: 2019

ISBN: 978-1-7339577-2-4

MRosales Novels
https://www.facebook.com/MRosalesNovels/

Chapter 1

As we de-board the plane, my anxiety begins to heighten. I look over at Jake and he gives me a pearly grin and I can see the excitement in his eyes. It's remarkable how fast one's life can change. Despite Jake's amnesia and inability to remember all the fond memories we once shared in the past, Jake wants to continue our engagement that never even occurred due to his faked death. As ecstatic as I am to finally be engaged to Jake, we still have quite a few obstacles in front of us before we can get married. One of the biggest obstacles being Jake's amnesia. Neither one us knew how long it would last or the long term effects it could cause. The important part is that we have each other again and even if he doesn't get his memory back, we will always have new memories ahead of us. Jake's mother is so sick in the head for trying to keep us a part by faking Jake's death. This leads me to our second biggest obstacle, our pending confrontation with Ms. Henson. Just the thought of it has me queasy to my stomach. If she would go to such extreme lengths to keep us apart, who knows what else she is capable of. I am glad that Jake is as pissed at his mom as I am. I can't imagine the hurt and betrayal he feels by having his own mother do something so cruel.

After we gather our bags, we catch a taxi and make our way to a hotel located just outside of our hometown.

We decided that it would be best to keep our distance from the town until we come up with a solid game plan. We agreed that it would be easier to approach my parents first and boy, I can just imagine the look they are going to give me. I hope we have a chance to fully explain ourselves before my mom whips out the phone to call Dr. Loucheski.

"You've been pretty quiet since we've gotten off the plane, is everything okay?" Jake asks me. "Yeah, I guess I am just a little nervous is all. It's been a couple months since this murderous alcoholic has been back home. Oh and let's not forget the whole reason we are here. To confront your mom who wanted to keep us apart so badly that she faked your death." He stops unpacking his bag and turns to me. "You have every right to be nervous, but everything is going to be okay. Besides you can't be labeled a murderous alcoholic anymore because if you haven't heard, I'm still alive. We are in this together and I'm not going to let you out of my sight." Jake has always had a way of comforting me at my worst times. I put my arms around his neck and gaze into his eyes, "You promise?" "I promise" he says and then gives me a kiss on the forehead. "How are we going to break it to your mom though?" I ask. "Uh, I'm not exactly sure. I haven't thought it through, but, I think we should definitely surprise her. Just show up and really shock the hell out of her. She's probably been freaking out since the guys told her I vanished from the airport." "True. That could work.

She can't run from us if we just show up. However, she does have a restraining order on me, so that would be a violation and I could go to jail if she calls the police." "Sarah, do you really think she will follow through with it, given the circumstances? If anything, I can threaten to call the police in return." "Good point. Then she will be forced to hear us out." "Exactly, and I think while we have her attention, it will be the perfect time to announce our engagement" Jake says. I hold out my left hand and admire the beautiful ring that now rests on my ring finger and have to refrain from giggling as I imagine Ms. Henson trying not to croak when we tell her the news. "Now we have one more very important matter to discuss" Jake says. "What's that?" "What the heck is for dinner? I am starving." I roll my eyes, "come on, there's a BBQ joint not too far from our hotel."

After dinner, we end up walking around Georgetown as Jake asks me questions about his past in hopes of filling in some blanks. His next questions shocks me though. "So who is my dad and where has he been during all this?" I could see why she would want him to forget about me, but I can't believe Ms. Henson is okay with letting her son forget about his own father. I get that it's a painful subject but still, it's not right. "Um, I'm really sorry Jake, but, your father died a year before you and your mom moved to Lexington. Your mom was looking for a fresh start and that's why you moved here." "Oh." I could see the look of sadness overtake his face. "How did he die? Do you know?" "Well, he was in the military and you had told me that he was deployed overseas on an undercover mission. Word got out that he was a spy and he was shot and killed." "That's terrible" he murmurs,"was I close with him?" "I can't really answer that. You had mentioned how he was gone a lot so it didn't feel like much of difference, but you were still heartbroken because you loved him and you two always got along when he was home." "Oh." Is all he says before a silence falls between us. I grab his hand and squeeze it tight. "I'm sorry" I tell him. "It's not your fault. It's just so damn frustrating that I can't remember anything, not even my own father." "I know babe, I know." I say as I give him a reassuring smile.

When we finally make it back to the hotel, we end up calling it a night as the food coma and jet-lag settles in. The past 48 hours have been a blur and still seems so unreal that I would be lying if said I wasn't leery of going to sleep in fear of waking up and it all being one big dream. I need to rest up though because tomorrow we are going to visit my parents and I can only pray it goes smoothly. As I'm drifting in and out of sleep, I come across an idea that I can't wait to share with Jake in the morning.

The next morning I roll over to Jake's side of the bed only to feel an empty spot. I jolt up and see the clock read 11:03am. How did I sleep in so late? "Jake" I call out, but there's no response. I quickly get out of bed and check the bathroom but there's still no sign of him. I start to panic. This is exactly what I was worried about. I begin pacing the room, trying to decide if I should turn on my cell-phone and try calling him. That would give our location away, if Ms. Henson's henchmen are still monitoring us. Beside's if they did take him, it's not like they would answer the phone and politely let me know their plans. I collapse on the bed, feeling defeated once again. As I'm laying there going over every worst possible scenario in my head, I hear someone at the door. "Who's there?" I shout as I grab the remote and hold it out in front of me as if I could actually defend myself with a remote. Jake walks in the room. "It's just me" he says. I drop the remote and run to embrace him. "You had me worried sick." "I'm sorry, I didn't think it would take that long." I didn't even have to ask where he had been. I take a step back and run my fingers through his fresh hair cut. "Do you like it?" He asks. "I love it, you look so handsome. I've just been used to seeing you with shaggy hair." "Well I'm glad to have that mop off my head. I hated having to grow it out." "Well now you don't have to." I say, followed by a kiss. "Did you sleep well?" He asks me. "I did, but I thought of something that I want to run by you." "Well, what is it?" "My therapist that I've told you about, what if you went to see him? Maybe he could help you in recalling your memories." "That's a great idea babe. I am desperate to try anything." "Great! We can contact him after we talk to my parents. That's if my mom doesn't call him as soon as we show up."

Chapter 2

We pull up to my parents and I can feel my heart beating a thousand miles an hour. We pay our driver and make our way up the porch. I knock twice before my father answers. "Sarah" he says with a puzzled expression and then his eyes dart to Jake and I can see him studying him intently as he looks him up and down. Jake's haircut makes it hard for my dad to deny what he was thinking. "Jake" he says slowly, as if he is questioning his own sanity. "Yes sir" Jake says as he sticks his hand out for a shake. My dad just stands there staring at him and then looks back at me. "Sarah, what is going on? Who is this?" "Dad, I can't wait to explain everything, but it's better if we do it one setting." He just nods and shouts over his shoulder, "Olivia, Haley, living room now." He steps aside to let us in and the three of us make our way to the living room.

Haley is already in the living room and does a double take as we walk in. "Oh my God" she says as she rises up from her seat. All four of us stand there silently, waiting for the last member of the party to show up. "Tony, what is so important" my mom says hastily as she emerges from around the corner. When we turn to face my mom, she stops dead in her tracks. "Wh..wh..what is the meaning of this? Who are you?" My mother questions as the skepticism fills her face. "Mom, Dad, Haley, this is

Jake." "The hell it is" my mother says snidely, "You are sick in the head Sarah" she says as she pulls out her cell phone. "It's true" Jake says looking directly at my mom and she lowers her phone. "If you could just give us a chance to explain" he adds. My mother looks at my dad and he gives us a nod and motions for us to sit down.

"That's impossible" my mom says after we finish explaining the situation. "Would your mother really go to such extremes?" My dad asks Jake. "It wouldn't surprise me," Haley scoffs, "no offense Jake." "None taken" he says before directing his attention to my dad. "I wish I could say it isn't so, but the way everything adds up, it makes it hard to deny." "But why? What was her reason for doing all of this? It seems so unnecessary" my mom says furiously. "Besides her thinking I'm not good enough for Jake and genuinely not liking me, we have no clue" I reply. My mom starts to cry. "Olivia what's wrong?" My dad asks. "Sarah, I have been so awful to you. I blamed you and I've been a terrible mother. I'm so sorry." I stand there silently, contemplating what to say. I can't tell her I forgive her, because even though I've been waiting for so long to hear her say those words, it doesn't mean she should be automatically forgiven. I also can't just say nothing. "Well it's in the past, let's focus on moving forward" I tell her. She nods as she wipes away the tears. "Now how about a group hug?" Jake suggests, so we all gather in for one big hug. "By the way, we have one more thing to tell you guys" Jake says. "Oh I don't think I can handle any more news today" my mom says rubbing her temples and plops down on the couch. I glance at Jake. "Show them" he tells me. I hold up my hand so they can see the ring. "We're engaged" I say giddily. Haley jumps up and comes over to me. "Wow, look at this thing!" Haley exclaims. Jake turns to my father, "I really hope, I asked your permission the first time." My dad chuckles, "You did. However, I didn't think you'd wait damn near a year to do it." "Wait, dad you knew?" "We both knew" he says as he puts his arm around my mom. "How come you never said anything?" I asked. "Well, we weren't sure at the time if he had asked you and thought it would make it harder to cope if you knew his intentions that night." And here I thought that I was holding onto this big secret this whole time. "Congratulations" my mom says as she gives me another hug. "Thanks mom." "So, when do we get to start planning?" Haley says rubbing her hands together mischievously. I let out a large sigh, "well we still have one big hurdle to clear first." "What's that?" My father asks. "We still have to confront Jake's mom." "You two are not going over there alone! Not after what you just told us" my father says sternly. "We have to dad. We have to catch her off guard." "Then we will go with you and we can wait in the car" my mom says and my dad nods in agreement. "Fair enough" Jake says. "Not today though, one day at a time" I say. Jake puts his arm around me, "agreed."

The next couple of hours we spend hanging out with my family and it reminds me of how things were before the accident and it makes me feel whole. My parents invite us to stay for dinner and retreat to the kitchen once we oblige and Haley goes up to her room to finish up some homework, leaving me and Jake alone. "Well, that went a lot better than we thought" Jakes says. "No kidding, now if only confronting your mom goes just as smooth." Jake gives me a doubtful look, "yeah, okay." "I know, wishful thinking. Do you think we should bring some sage to help ward off the demon inside your mom?" Jake laughs, "I don't think it'll help much" he says and then gives me a kiss.

After dinner my parents insist that we spend the night, but we politely decline so my dad offers to drive us to our hotel instead. Before we leave, we ask my mom to set up an appointment in two days for Jake with Dr. Loucheski. Lord knows he's going to need it, especially the day after we confront his mom. When my dad drops us off we change into our pj's and cuddle up in bed.

"Today was nice" Jake says. "It really was" I tell him. "It felt familiar. I feel like I've known them forever." "Well you kinda have" I chuckle. "You know what I mean silly. It just makes me sad that we won't get that same feeling with my mom. It's not fair that your parents are so accepting of me, then for my mom to treat you so poorly."

"Nothing worth having comes easy babe." "This is true" he says. I could feel him looking down at me so I look up at him, "What?" "You're beautiful, that's what." I lean up to give him a kiss and he holds me there so our kiss lingers for just a moment and I can feel a warm tingly sensation erupt through my entire body. As much as I crave Jake, he's not the same Jake that I've been with before and I want for our next, first time to be special. I assume he feels the same way, because despite us having a hotel room all to ourself, he hasn't been as adamant as he was before we discovered the truth. I return my head to the spot on his chest and we stay there for another hour watching TV before we decide to go to bed.

The next morning we are slow to get up, dreading what lies ahead for the day. Today we are confronting Jake's mom and my nerves already have me picking at my cuticles. Jake rolls over and grabs my hands. "Hey, it's gonna be okay" he tells me and gives me a reassuring smile. "I know, I know. I'm just ready to get this over with" "Me too babe. Speaking of, what time are your parents going to pick us up?" "They said around 10:30." Jake yawns and stretches out his arms before getting out of bed, "welp, we better start getting ready then." "Ugh, I don't wanna," I groan. "Too bad," Jake says as he starts to tickle me. I burst with laughter and quickly roll out of bed, "Okay, okay I'm up!" He pulls me to him and gives me a long kiss. "You know we could save time and shower together" Jake says with a wink. I could feel myself blush as I quickly look away from his lustful gaze. "I think that would end up taking more time." I say as I breakaway and start gathering my things. "Fine, I guess you can go first then." "Already planned on it." I tell him as I shut the bathroom door.

Chapter 3

The ride to Ms. Henson's house is for the most part silent. When we finally pull up, my parents turn around to face us. "Are you sure you don't want us to come with you?" My mother asks. "No mom, I think we'll be okay. If it gets too bad we will just leave." I tell her. She gives me a nod. "Good luck" my father tells us. We exit the car and make our way up the drive way.

When we make it to the door, we pause and look at one another. Jake gently pushes my hair behind my ear and gives a half smile. I return the smile and then Jake rings the doorbell. My heart begins to beat faster and I instantly become nauseous when I hear Ms. Henson yell "coming." As she opens the door her jaw suddenly drops and she quickly corrects herself and displays an attitude of ignorance. She directs her glare at me, "What is the meaning of this, who is this?" "Oh cut the crap, you know who this is" I say angrily. Her jaw drops once again. "How dare you speak to me that way. You shouldn't even be within one hundred feet of me you little brat." I look at Jake. "Mom, just stop. Let us in so we can talk about this" he tells her. She looks at the both of us and then looks back at Jake with tearful eyes. "You can come in, but she is not welcome" she finally says. "Then I'm not welcomed either" he says while taking my hand and then turns to leave. "Jason! I mean Jake, wait!" Ms. Henson shouts. I knew it, I think to myself. We stop walking and turn to face her once more. "Both of you can come in" she says, stepping aside to let us in.

The three of us take a seat in the living room as an awkward silence falls upon us. "Mom" Jake says slowly, "we already know what you did, but could you tell us why?" Her eyes dart to me and she begins to shift in her sit. "I don't think this is the right time to discuss this" she says. "If we have this discussion now instead of drawing it out then we can try to move past this and start fresh" I tell her. "She's right mom. The sooner we get this conversation out of the way, the sooner we can put all this behind us." "It's not that simple" she tell us, "I don't think you understand what I've done." "Oh I think we understand clearly" I say. She gives me an evil smirk, "sweetie, if only you knew." "Don't call me 'sweetie'" I say angrily. "You're in my home, I can do whatever I please" she tells me snarkily. "Isn't that the type of attitude that's gotten you into this mess?" I reply. "Ladies" Jake says breaking up the growing hostility. "Sorry" I mutter. "Mom, we just want to understand why you would do something so extreme to keep us apart? It was cruel and selfish of you to interfere with our relationship. I mean to fake my death just to keep us from being with each other, that's pretty drastic." "I did it because I love you and I care about you. Sarah will never be good enough for you and I wish you could see that. I didn't want you to make a huge mistake that you'd regret." I could feel the tears start to form in my eyes. I always knew how Ms. Henson felt about me just by the way she treated me, but to actually hear her say it aloud, hurt. "Mistake that I would regret? Are you talking about how I was going to propose?" Jake asks. Ms. Henson becomes pale, "Propose what on earth are you talking about?" She asks horrified. "The night of the accident, I was going to propose to Sarah, that's where we were headed when we got into the wreck." "Lies!" Ms. Henson shouts, "You would've told me. Sarah is just taking advantage of your memory loss." "That is not true, I would never lie about such a thing!" I yell back. "Do you recall this on your own Jake? Or is she the one who told you? How much of that night do you remember?" Ms. Henson asks frantically. "How much do I remember? I can't even remember my own father. You want to talk about someone manipulating me, how about we start with you. You lied to me and pretended that I was a whole other person and fed me a bunch of lies about my past that I couldn't remember. It doesn't matter if she told me or not. We love each other mom and if this miracle of fate doesn't prove to you that we deserve to be together then I don't know what to tell you other than you better get use to it because we are engaged" Jake says. Despite sitting down, Ms. Henson has to steady herself. "You're what?"

She asks hysterically. Jake grabs my left wrist and holds it up for her to see the ring on my hand, "We're engaged" he tells her firmly. "This can't be, I won't allow it." "You have no choice" Jake says as he stands up and pulls me to a standing position too. "Where are you going?" Ms. Henson asks. "We are leaving, because this conversation is over" he says. "Where will you be staying? When can I see you again?" She starts to cry. Seriously, she's going to cry like she's the victim here. "You can see us at the airport, when leave to go back to California." Ms. Henson gives him a bewildered look and I can't help but be shocked by his response too. We have not discussed any details of what we planned to do after today. "California? If you know the truth, why would you go back there? I can't lose you again, I just got you back" she croaks. "So you can't meddle in our lives" I say, in which Ms. Henson shoots me an icy glare. Jake put his arm around me and pulls me close. "What difference does it make? If I never found out, I'd still be in California, clueless to your lies and pretending to be someone I'm not anyway." Ms. Henson follows us to the door while trying to pull herself together. Before opening the door, Jake pauses and turns around one last time, "Oh and mom, do not interfere with our relationship anymore, or you will never hear from me again. Your lies and games are over from here on out." Jake's words shock his mother as she gasps and covers her mouth. He then opens the door and I follow him out, but before I make it out the doorway Ms. Henson leans into my ear and whispers "Looks like you'll never know the truth." I quickly turn to face her, but she slams the door in my face. I turn back around to see Jake already up the driveway. "You coming?" He asks and I nod my head. What did she mean by that? Why would she whisper it just to me, instead of telling us both? Looks like she hasn't changed one bit and I had a feeling despite Jake's demand, her lies and games were nowhere near over.

Chapter 4

The Jake I knew before the accident would have never stood up to his mother that way. We always had to be cautious of her feelings and pick and choose what we told her. It makes me wonder since Jake had not told her his intentions of proposing to me that night, how we would have pulled off our engagement. We most likely would have had to keep it a secret until the time was right. After all, that's what we had to do with everything else in our relationship at that time. Maybe this accident is a blessing in disguise. Now me and Jake are a united front and stronger than ever and it's all his mother's doing. However, I am impatient to get back to the hotel so we can discuss our plans going forward. I had not thought about going back to California, but apparently that's what Jake wants to do.

After recapping the discussion we had with Ms. Henson to my parents over lunch they bring us back to the hotel so we can decompress. "Jake, now that your mother knows, do you think it would be okay if you two to turn on your cellphones so we can get ahold of you?" My mother asks as we get out of the car. "Of course, I don't think it's an issue now" he says. "Great. I'll give you a call in the morning Sarah." I give her a nod and they drive off.

When we make it up to the room, we collapse on the bed and lay there in silence for a moment. "Jake." "Yeah?" "Are we really going back to California?" Jake rolls onto his side to face me, "Well, why not? We are already established out there, and let's not forget that I am dead to everyone here anyway. It will be too hard and embarrassing to try and explain to everyone we know what happened. Not to mention, I can't even remember anyone anyway. I think we would be better off starting fresh out there." He has a point, it's not like we could pick up where we left off here with no questions asked. To everyone we know, Jake is dead and it wouldn't be an easy thing to explain every time someone recognized him. "Alright. Whatever you want." I tell him. He pulls me close and gives me a kiss. "Now that we got the hard part out of the way, we can finally move forward and start planning the wedding." I sit up fast, "Really?" I say excitedly. "Well yeah, there's nothing holding us back now" he says as he gives me his heart melting smile. I let out a shriek and climb on top of him as I smother him with kisses. He laughs and then gazes into my eyes, "I love seeing you so happy" he tells me. "I'm just so excited! Can you believe we are getting married?" "No, actually, I can't believe it, because I have to be the luckiest guy in the world to end up with the most beautiful fiancé inside and out." "Every guy says that" I say crossing my arms and giving him a playful frown. "Okay, but how many can prove it by finding his way back to the love of his life despite all the odds?" He says, raising an eyebrow. "Just one" I say giving him a kiss on the lips.

The next morning I wake up and I can hear Jake already in the shower. He has always been an early bird, whereas I could sleep till noon if you let me. Shoot, I forgot to turn on my phone last night. My mom has probably called a dozen times already. As my phone turns on, all my missed messages and notifications send my phone into a buzzing frenzy. My heart skips a beat when I see Thomas's name come across my phone. I had been so caught up in everything with Jake that I never thought about what it meant for me and Thomas. I guess I thought when I ran away with Jake that it would mean I could just runaway from my relationship with Thomas and leave it all behind.

I press play on the voicemail Thomas left me yesterday. "Um, hey Sarah, it's Thomas again. I was worried when you missed school and weren't answering any of my texts or calls so I tried to go check on you at your grandparents today, but they said you weren't there and weren't sure when or if you'd be back. I hope you're okay and I just want to apologize if any of this is my fault. I know I've been distance lately and I hope that it didn't push you away, because the truth is, I've been trying to find the right way to tell you this, but, I love you Sarah. I've just been so scared of my feelings and I should have just been a man and told you in person when I first realized it. Anyways, if you could give me a call, I'd really like to hear from you…"

"Who's that?" Jake asks, startling me and causing me to drop my phone. "Oh, um, just an old voicemail from my mom." Why did I feel the need to lie? Jake is my fiancé now and he knows we were both in on going relationships before we left to come here and have unfinished business to tend to. After all, he probably has similar messages from Stacy. It does make me feel anxious to know that when we return to California I will have to break Thomas's heart once and for all, and his newly expressed feelings aren't going to make this any easier. "Oh, has she called this morning yet?" "Surprisingly not, maybe I should just call her and get it out of the way" I tell him. "Good idea."

When I call my mom, she tells me that she set up an appointment later today with Dr. Loucheski and Jake. Dr. Loucheski wants it to be one on one, so mom plans for me, her, and Haley to go wedding dress shopping while they meet. "And so it begins" Jake says teasingly as I get off the phone. I roll my eyes, "I don't get how I am supposed to pick out a dress when we don't even have a date picked out yet." "Well maybe we should work on picking a date tonight then." "Alright" I say, giving him a big smile. I have dreamed about my wedding since I was a little girl and to know that the time is finally here, it felt surreal. There is so much planning to do though.

Haley and my mom came to pick us up around three and when we drop Jake off I couldn't deny that I was nervous letting him out of my sight. Could anyone blame me though? I walk him into Dr. Loucheski's office and we share a long hug before we part ways. I really hope this visit is beneficial for Jake's sake. He hides it well, but I know it bother's him not being able to remember things. As I make my way back to the car, the excitement settles in and when I get in the car my mom and Haley turn to me and we all three let out an excited squeal. "What kind of dress do you have in mind?" Haley asks. "I was thinking a strapless with a sweetheart neckline for sure." "You are going to look so beautiful" mom comments.

After an hour and a half of looking and trying on dresses, I find the one. It is an off white, A-line style dress with some bling on the form fitting top half and a train that is easy to manage. "This is it, this is the one" I say as I give my mom and Haley a 360 degree twirl. My mom lets a tear fall as she approaches to give me a hug. "You look gorgeous sis, the off white really flatters your skin tone and now I see why you wanted the sweetheart neckline, it really suits your assets" Haley says giving me wink. "Thanks" I say as I let out a laugh at the fact she is referring to my breasts as assets. "Are you going to get it now?" My mother asks. "I don't know, we don't even have a date picked out yet, I feel a little silly even trying on dresses." "Oh pish posh, I say you get it. They may not have it later." "She's got a point" Haley adds. "Fine. I'll get it, but you are going to have to hold onto it for me so Jake doesn't see it." "Deal" my mom says quickly.

We stop by my parents to drop off the dress before we go pick up Jake. Then when we pull up, Jake is already finished and waiting outside for us. "Sorry, we got a little carried away" I tell Jake as he gets in the car. "Carried away? You mean you picked out your wedding dress" Haley says excitedly. I give Jake an awkward smile, hoping he doesn't think I am trying to rush things. "That's great. I already know you are going to look stunning" he says. Haley sticks her finger in her mouth and makes a barfing sound. "Oh hush" I tell her playfully. "How did your appointment go?" I ask Jake. "Not bad. Dr. Loucheski says next time we can try some exercises that may help me recall some of my memories. He says we can't do it all at once because it's too mentally exhausting, but we can do it little by little." "That's great news. When do you see him again?" "Well, actually, I'm not going to see him. I told him we are heading back to California and he said that wouldn't be a bad idea given the circumstances. So, our first few appointments are going to be recorded over Skype and then he wants to set me up with a local psychiatrist in California." "Oh, well, I guess that's good right?" "Yeah, I just hope I can benefit from the exercises. He says they aren't guaranteed, but it's worth a shot." "I know babe" I say as I rest my head on his shoulder.

Back at the hotel, me and Jake begin discussing wedding dates and other details pertaining to the wedding. We agree that since we are going back to California we need to wait and finish out the semester first, so we decide on January 4th for our wedding date. It is also mutually decided that we just have a small ceremony with just immediate family and grandparents, given the circumstances. "You realize my mom is going to burst with excitement when I tell her that we've decided on a date?" I tell him. "And you realize my mom is probably going to burst into flames?" He replies. We both laugh. "I'm sorry that you've chosen such a heathen to marry" I say jokingly. Jake's face turns serious, "Don't ever apologize for my love for you. I will always love you, and even then that's not enough." I pull his face to mine and kiss his soft lips. As our kiss lingers, he guides me down onto the bed and I start to kiss along his neck. I slip my hands under his shirt and I feel the same familiar muscular body that I have been longing for. He pulls his shirt off with one hand while the other slides underneath me and pulls my body to his. He pulls my hair to one side as he trades kisses between each side of my neck. "Take it off" he whispers. His warm breath in my ear sends goosebumps all over my body. I do as he says and I take off my shirt as he unhooks my bra. I let his lips roam their way down my body and my body begins to tremble when he makes it to stomach. I am about to encourage him to keep going when a sudden knock at the door startles both of us. Whoever is on the other side of that door has poor choice of timing.

"Go get the door" I hiss. "I can't" he says reluctantly as he points towards a noticeable bulge in his pants. "Just a second" I shout as I fumble to put my shirt back on. As I open the door my smile fades, "Mary, what are you doing here?" I question. How did Jake's mom find out where we were staying? "Mom?" Jake says inquisitively as he comes from abound the corner. "I'm sorry to drop by like this, I hope I didn't interrupt anything" she says. "Actually you did" I reply feeling more sexually frustrated than ever. "Um, well may I come in?" She asks. "I think you're fine where you're at as I'm sure this won't be a long visit" Jake says. Ms. Henson gives a nod, "I just wanted to say I am sorry for how I reacted yesterday and I think both of you are right. We need to put the past behind us and I want to put my best foot forward from here on out, if you'll just give me the chance." Jake looks at me with a hopeful smile, "What do you say?" He asks me. Every fiber of my being tells me not to trust her, but when I look into Jake's eyes at how happy it makes him to see his mom's new found acceptance then I know I'd be the bad guy standing between him and his mom. "Sure, but you're gonna have to prove it with time. Forgiveness isn't something you can just shut on and off" I tell Mary. "Oh thank you, I won't let you down" Ms. Henson says as she gives each of us a hug. "Anywho, that's all I wanted to say, I'll be going now" she says and then walks off.

I shut the door slowly and then turn to face Jake. His face is beaming as if he just won't the lottery. "Can you believe it? My mom has finally come to accept you! I think our conversation with her worked" Jake says excitedly. "Babe, don't you think it's a little suspicious though? For one, she shows up here, unannounced, and we didn't even tell her where we were staying. And two, she proclaims to have dropped a hatred that she has had for me for years, just like that and now wants to be buddies?" "Maybe she just realizes that she can't fight it anymore and if she wants to keep me in her life then she has to change her ways." "Yeah, maybe" I say. Jake has always sought out the good in everyone, and with it being his mother of all people I'm not sure if he is just being gullible or if his ability to see how outrageous this seems is obscured by his love for his mom. It is clever on Ms. Henson's part though, to pretend like we are on good terms that way if anything were to go down between us I would be the trouble maker.

Chapter 5

Shortly after Jake's mother left last night, we came to the conclusion that it was time for us to head back to California. Which is why, we are currently navigating our way through the packed airport to get to our terminal. Despite how eager I am to get back to California so me and Jake can move on with our lives, I am also a nervous wreck thinking about how I'm going to break things off with Thomas. I don't know if I'll be able to stand in front of him and crush his heart. "Wanna wait here while I go get us something to eat?" Jake asks me. "Sure, grab me a water too, please." "You got it" he says and leans down to give me a kiss.

Not long after Jake leaves I get a call from Stacy, but I reject it. She calls back immediately, I let out a sigh, knowing full well I am going to regret answering her call, but I do it anyway. "Hey Stacy" "Sarah, where on earth are you? I haven't seen or heard from you or Jason in days. Is he with you?" I take a hard swallow, I really shouldn't be the one to tell her, but I can't keep lying to her." "Um, actually he is. And Stacy, I really hope you can forgive me, but there's something you have to understand when I tell you this." "I think I'm going to be sick" Stacy says sharply. "Stacy, Jason isn't who you think he is. His real name is Jake and he's my boyfriend, the one I told you about that I thought died." "You are seriously messed up in the head Sarah. I think you're just bitter and psycho" Stacy says hatefully. "Thomas wasn't enough for you, you had to have Jason too. You knew he liked you and you took advantage of it. How could you?" "It's not even like that Stacy, I promise." "Your promises mean nothing to me anymore." "Stacy please, just listen. We love each other and I didn't want to be the one to tell you this, let alone over the phone, but we are engaged now." "Not after I tell him the good news" she says and then hangs up.

Good news? What could she possibly mean by that? I feel like every time we start to move forward there's something or someone that drags us back down. Jake approaches me with a bottle of water and a burger. "Everything okay?" He asks me. "I suppose. I just got a call from Stacy." "Did you answer?" I nod my head. "What did she say?" "She said we aren't going to be together once she tells you the good news." "What's the good news?" He asks. "I don't know, maybe you should call her" I tell him. Jake grabs my hand and gives it a squeeze. I look into his eyes as he speaks. "Sarah, nothing could change the way I feel about you, if that's what you're worried about." "I am more worried about her splitting us up" I say. "That's not going to..." before he can finish his sentence, his phone rings. He pulls his phone out to reveal that it's Stacy calling. Jake looks at me for approval. "Might as well get it over with" I say.

"Hello. Whoa Stacy, calm down. I can't understand you when you're yelling." It's killing me not being able to hear what she's saying, but I'm sure Jake will let me know. "Yes, I know. If you could just give me a chance to apologize. I'm really sorry Stacy, it was never my intention to lead you on, but I'm with Sarah now. Of course I care about you, it's just complicated. Wait, what did you just say? Are you positive? When did you find out? Ok, um thanks for letting me know, but I gotta go." She must have told him and I'm not sure if I'm ready to hear the news. Jake's tone turns tense, "I don't know Stacy, we will talk later, I have to process this. I said I don't know, I'll call you later."

He hangs up the phone and rests his face into his hands. I gently put my hand on his shoulder, "Jake" I say compassionately. "She's pregnant Sarah" Jake blurts out. I feel like I'm going to be sick. I stand up and Jake grabs my hand, "Please, don't leave." I break free from his grip and run to the bathroom. Just as I make it in the stall the tears begin to fall. I don't know how to feel. Apparently their relationship was more advanced than I thought. I feel heartbroken. This changes everything, it's not like we can just go get married after finding out he got another girl pregnant. Jake's morals will push him to do the right thing and that's to be with Stacy. That way the kid doesn't grow up without a father. Even though Jake doesn't remember his father, his morals haven't changed. Before the accident we had always talked about our future and even though I told him I wasn't ready for kids for awhile, he expressed to me that when we finally had kids he didn't want to be an absent father since he knew what it felt like growing up with a father that was only half there. I could feel my whole world starting to crumble, even if he chose to stay with me, how could I in good faith let him, knowing that I would be the reason the kid grows up in a broken home. The selfish part of me knows I won't be able to share Jake with Stacy for the rest of our lives and I start to get angry. How could he be so stupid?

I pull myself together when I hear that our flight is starting to board. I contemplate on missing the flight and just staying here, but that's not going to solve any of my problems. Besides, then I'd have to call my parents and explain to them how much more twisted and humiliating my life just became. I exit the bathroom and Jake is anxiously waiting outside. "Sarah, I don't even know where to begin." "Not now" I say sharply. I grab my bag from him and get in line to board the plane. Once we are seated, I put my headphones in and turn to stare out the window. After 30 minutes of giving Jake the silent treatment, I finally decide I want some answers.

I nudge Jake, "are you awake?" "Yeah, I can't sleep" he says. "How far along is she?" "She said she hasn't had an official appointment yet but she's guessing seven or eight weeks." I can feel the lump in my throat start to form. "So I take it there's a possibility since you're taking it so hard." Jake lets out a heavy sigh, "The night of Thomas's party, after I saw you two hooking up, I was hurt, really hurt Sarah. I got pretty wasted and Stacy kept pushing herself on me and I was a fool and caved in. It didn't mean anything, I swear." "Well it's about to mean a whole lot" I tell him before continuing, "we didn't even have sex that night. Thomas stopped it because he didn't want to take advantage of me while I was drunk." Jake is silent as he clenches his jaw and I can see the regret in his face. "I'm such an idiot. How could I be so careless?" "Was that the only time?" I ask sternly. "Yes, I promise. It was just that one time and I instantly regretted it the next morning." Jake tries to hold my hand, but I pull it away. The thought of him touching her and being with her in that way makes me feel betrayed. Neither one of us had been with anyone besides each other and it hurt to know that Jake had been with someone else. I know we weren't together, but in my mind we were and I can't help but feel as if I had been cheated on. I couldn't be any more pissed at Jake's mother, this is all her fault. "Please don't do this. I love you Sarah." "How can we realistically be together now?" I say coldly. "We can figure something out. It doesn't mean we can't be together." "Really? You should probably tell Stacy that." We both fall silent and we stay that way the rest of the flight.

Chapter 6

We make it to Jake's apartment and he gets out to get the bags. "Leave mine" I say. "What, why? I thought you were going to stay with me now." "I don't think that's such a good idea anymore" I tell him. Jake comes around to my side and opens the door, "Sarah, please don't push me away. We will get through this." I start to cry, "Everything is ruined" I choke out. I felt awkward crying in front of Hector, but it wouldn't be the first time. Jake gives me a pleading look and drops to his knees. I run my fingers through his hair as I think to myself. If we weren't meant to be together then why would fate bring us back to each other just for it pull us apart again? I undo my seatbelt and Jake looks up to me with a face of relief. "You're on probation" I tell him. He scoops me up out of the car and twirls me around before setting me down. "Whatever it takes, just as long as I don't lose you."

It was eery being back in Jake's apartment, but we needed to work things out and it's not like we could stay at my grandparents. I figure I can avoid our discussion a little longer by calling my parents to tell them we made it back, but that conversation didn't last long. Now we were both sitting in awkward silence on his couch. "So who are you going to call first? Stacy or your mom? I'm sure your mom will be pleased to know the news." "Sarah can you please stop with the hostility. You're not the only one that's having to process this." He's right. I'm just as scared of losing him, as he is of losing me, but I'm hurt. "I'm sorry" I mutter. "I'm not telling my mom anything until I talk to Stacy." "Okay." "Do you want to go with me to meet Stacy?" "I don't think that's such a good idea" I tell him. "You aren't going to be able to avoid her forever. Besides she's going to have to get use to the idea of us being together." "Fine" I reply.

Stacy suggests meeting at a smoothie shop and I don't think Jake told her that I will be tagging along, so, I can't wait to see how this goes. By time we pull up, I think I have chewed my nails down to nubs. I just pray she doesn't cause a scene. "Maybe you should just go in." "Don't be silly, we are a team" Jake says and gives me a kiss on the forehead. When we approach the shop I can see Stacy sitting at a table already slurping down a smoothie. I don't see a baby bump, but I have to remind myself she's not that far along anyway.

"Hi Stacy." "Jason!" She shouts and throws her arms around him and starts to cry into his shoulder. I instantly regret coming and start to feel severely out of place. Jake slowly pulls her arms off of him and she wipes away her tears. "My name isn't Jason, it's Jake" he tells her. "What is she doing here?" She asks, oblivious to what he just said. "Stacy, she's my fiancé. We've both come to talk about the situation at hand." "You're seriously still going to marry her after what I've told you?" "Yes, I do. I love her" he says as he pulls me to his side. "What about me?

What about our baby?" "I care about you a lot Stacy, but I don't think I could ever feel the same way about you as I do for Sarah. As far as our baby goes, I will love him or her unconditionally and I will always be there for them." Stacy gives me a smug look, "Well it looks like you need to figure out what it is you want, because if you're still with Sarah by time the baby comes, you won't be apart of their life." "Stacy, you can't be serious?" Jake says astonished. If she wasn't pregnant I would've slapped her right in the face. Who does she think she is giving him an ultimatum like that? "Oh, but I am. I'm not saying we have to run to the alter, but you can either be there for me and the baby or you can be with Sarah, your choice. You don't get to just play with peoples feelings and expect no repercussions." "You are such a bitch" I say to Stacy. "Maybe, but you're not the one knocked up by your so called boyfriend who ran away to be with your best-friend." I clench my teeth trying not to let get my emotions get the best of me, because in reality she had a point. I would be bitter too. "This isn't right Stacy. Making a demand like this, it isn't going to make me fall in love with you." "Maybe not right away," she says as she runs her hand down his chest, "But maybe you could ponder on the night we made our baby and remember how badly you wanted me then. How much you loved every inch of my body" she says giving me taunting smirk. I can't listen to anymore of this and if I stay I'll end up getting into a physical altercation and I just couldn't chance it. I run out the door and I can hear Jake call out for me. I don't stop running till I make it to the end of the pier. I knew it, I knew this would happen. I could feel my heart shattering into a billion pieces and I have no idea what to do. So, I make an impulse decision that will make it easier on everyone. I pull out my phone to make a call.

Thomas pulls up and I flash him a nervous smile. I haven't really thought this through, but all I know is I'm not going to be the reason Jake doesn't get to be apart of his kids life. "Hi" I say while giving a small wave. "Hi" Thomas replies. "We need to talk" I tell him. His demeanor turns gloomy as he gives me a nod. "Can we go to your place?" I ask him and he gives me a confused look. "I don't want to be home right now and I'm not sure where else to go" I say as I start to break down. Thomas quickly gets out of the car and hurries to my side. "Okay, whatever you want. Just please don't cry, it hurts me to see you like this" Thomas says as he opens the passenger door.

Convincing Thomas's parents to let me stay the night is easier than I thought. They probably feel sorry for me since I look like a total train wreck. When we make it up to his room he lends me a shirt and some shorts to change into. After I change, I curl up next to Thomas on his bed. He doesn't say anything, as I let the sniffles commence. We sit in silence while he plays with my hair and it's not long before I fall asleep. Between jet lag and the mental exhaustion, I am wore out.

The next morning I wake up with seven missed calls and twenty texts from Jake. I set my phone back down and roll over. "Good morning" Thomas says. Not going to lie, I had gotten use to waking up next to Jake and this morning threw me for a loop. "Good morning" I reply. "How did you sleep?" He asks. "Alright." "You think you're up for talking now?" Thomas asks. "I guess so" I say reluctantly. "If not, it's okay" he tells me. "No, we need to. I'm just afraid that you are going to hate me after I explain everything." Thomas brushes aside the hair in my eyes and stares at me for just a moment, "I might get upset, but I don't think I could ever hate you" he says. "Well, I want to start off by saying that I care about you so much. I didn't think I'd ever be able to care about someone other than Jake, but then you came along." "Sarah if you're feeling pressured because I told you I love you then don't worry. I'm not expecting you to be on the same page so quickly." "No that's not it. Please just let me finish." He gives me a nod and I continue, "I thought Jake was gone. I was under the impression that he died, but apparently he didn't. His mom faked his death. Trust me, I know how unbelievable this sounds, but it's true. What's even crazier is that, I found him. I had no clue at first since he was under witness protection and suffering from amnesia, but one of the guys protecting him felt bad and told me. It's Jason. Jason has been Jake this whole time and we went to Kentucky to confront his mom and discovered the truth." I pause for a moment to give Thomas time to process what I have said. "So… Jason is actually Jake. Which is your ex-boyfriend that you thought died in the car accident." "Correct" I say. "How long have you known? Have you two been seeing each other behind my back?" "I just found out a couple days ago, that's why I vanished. We needed to confront his mom in Kentucky. And no, not necessarily. You have to understand, there's a lot of history between us and finding out he was still alive brought up a lot of emotions. The last he knew we were engaged and that's where he wanted to continue things" I tell him as I hold up my hand to reveal the ring on my hand. Thomas lets out a sigh and rolls onto his back and stares at the ceiling. "I wanted to tell you, but I had to make sure it was even true first. I hope you'll be able to forgive me." "I forgive you Sarah. After all, it's not like I could blame you given the history between you two. I'm more frustrated with the situation. I finally fall in love with an amazing girl and her boyfriend comes back from the dead to take her away from me. I guess Jessica was right, karma would catch up with me eventually." "Not quite" I say. Thomas gives me a puzzled expression. "There's more. As you know, Jason and Stacy were dating prior to us finding out the truth and last night when we made it back she broke the news that she's pregnant." The last words choke me up and Thomas pulls me close to him. "I'm sorry" he whispers to me. It felt good to confide in Thomas about this and for him to be so understanding only reassured me that I was making the right decision. "Thomas, I know I don't deserve you, but I still want to be with you. If you'll still have me that is." Thomas hesitates to respond and I couldn't blame him. How could he even trust me? Especially around Jake. "She's just pregnant. That doesn't mean you two can't be together, it's not like old times where he's forced to marry her." I let out a large huff. "Let me guess, there's more?" Thomas says and I give him a nod. "Stacy gave Jake the ultimatum of being with me or being in the kids life and I don't want to force Jake to make that decision." "Ah, I see" Thomas says. I sit up quickly at the realization of what I just said. "Thomas, that does not mean I'm wanting to be with you by default. Like I said, I care about you a lot and I don't think I could handle losing two people I really care about. I know it may seem like I'm running back to you because things didn't work out with Jake, but that's not true. You were the first person I wanted to call when I found out and I did. I choose you." The last part may be a small lie, but what else am I supposed to say to convince him to stay with me? If I run back to Thomas willingly then it'll make it easier on Jake to make his decision, and if he thinks I'm happy with Thomas then hopefully it won't make Jake feel as guilty. I don't exactly want him and Stacy to be together, but if that's the way things play out then so be it. It's not like I can be the only that gets to move on. "This definitely changes some things, but it doesn't change the way I feel about you" Thomas finally says. Thomas looks me in the eyes and gives me a kiss before continuing, "If you want to try and make this work then I'm willing to give us the chance. But I have to say, I don't think I feel comfortable with you and Jake being alone together given your history." "I understand" is all I say. I don't know how well I can uphold that promise but it's not like he's saying I can't ever see him again. Never in my life did I think I would see myself breaking up with Jake and I know it's going to break my heart in a million pieces. "Please just bear with me, this is a difficult time for me." "I know" Thomas says as he gets up and starts to get dressed. "Want to get some breakfast?" I suggest. "That sounds great" Thomas says while flashing me a big smile.

Chapter 7

I knew it was inevitable before I would have to talk to Jake, after all, I have to get my things from his place. Which is why after breakfast, Thomas and I stop by Jake's apartment to get my stuff. I convince Thomas to let me go up alone, this is going to be hard enough, I don't need an audience. I knock on the door, hoping that he is here since I didn't think to ask beforehand. Jake opens the door and I can see his red blood shot eyes with dark circles underneath and I know it's because he has been crying. I instantly feel terrible. He quickly pulls me into a hug as he starts to cry.

"I didn't know when I'd see you next" Jake says as he squeezes me a little tighter. I knew the longer we embraced, the harder it would be for me to do what I came here to do. "Jake…I'm sorry" I say as I gently push him away and my own tears start to fall. "For what? If anyone should be sorry it's me" he replies. Our eyes meet for a split second, but I quickly push past him to go grab my things. "Wait, Sarah, what are you doing?" "We can't do this Jake. I'm not going to stand between you and your kid." "Sarah, we can work this out. I can take her to court, she can't legally keep the baby away from me." "At what cost? Thousands of dollars or her lying to the kid to turn it against you too? What happens when your mom finds out? Whose side do you think she'll be on? Every corner you turn your going to be pressured to be with Stacy and I don't think I could handle it" I sob. "Who cares? I love you and I don't want lose you again." I make my way back to the door with my things, "I've got to go. Thomas is waiting for me" I say. "Thomas? You've got to be joking?" "No. I spent the night with him last night and told him everything. Surprisingly he's willing to still make our relationship work." "Are you serious? What about making us work?" He yells. "It won't work" I tell him firmly. "What if we keep it a secret?" He says desperately. I turn to face him, "A secret!" I shout, "So what? A secret we keep for the rest of our lives. A secret that won't allow us to realistically be together. We wouldn't even be able to get married" I say as I take off my ring and shove it in his hand. "Please don't do this. I love you Sarah" he says with tears rolling down his face. "Goodbye Jake" I say and quickly exit the apartment.

I rest against the door to his apartment and let the tears fall. I can feel my heart sink to the pit of my stomach and it makes me nauseous. I wipe away my tears the best I can and make my way down the stairs with my things. When I make it back to the car, Thomas doesn't say anything he just takes my things from me and puts them in the trunk. I didn't tell him where to take me, but I think he knew where I needed to go. We pull up to my grandparents and I give him a look of defeat. "I guess I have to face them sometime" I say. "I can come in with you so you're not alone?" Thomas suggests. "No, that's okay. This is something I need to do on my own and they'll probably be pretty confused as it is." "Okay babe." I hesitate to get out of the car and Thomas takes my hand, "You are strong and you are going to get through this. We are going to get through this" he tells me. I give him a weak smile, "Yes we will" I say and then get out out of the car.

I didn't feel like it was appropriate to just barge into my grandparents so I ring the doorbell and wait to be invited in. "Oh Sarah!" My grandma exclaims as she opens the door. She hugs me and then gives me a puzzled expression. "Where is Jake? Your mom already called and told us everything" she says excitedly. I do my best to keep from crying, it's not like she knows. "Not everything" I tell her. "What do you mean?" She asks. "Maybe you should get grandpa. I don't know how many times I'll be able to explain this" I tell her.

After I finish telling my grandparents the latest tragedy in my life, I retreat to my previously claimed room. I begin to wonder if this is karma for cheating on Thomas and it certainly feels that way. I only have myself to blame though. I pressured Jake to be with Stacy because I was too afraid of breaking up with Thomas. Now look where I'm at. I need to quit thinking about him. Ugh, and I still need to tell my parents. Maybe I can call Haley and tell her and she can just tell them for me. That would be the less embarrassing option. Part of me wonders what Ms. Henson's reaction will be. Will she be happy that Jake is moving on with someone other than me or will she be just as cruel to Stacy? Surely the thought of having a grandchild would defrost some of her frozen heart.

When I get off the phone with Haley, my head is pounding. I am mentally exhausted. Over the past three days I have went from being re-engaged to the love of my life that I thought was dead, to getting told he's having a baby with a chick who is technically his girlfriend, and then to breaking up with my fiancé to be with my boyfriend so it's easier on everyone. My life is such a mess. I force myself to get up and go take a bubble bath, hoping that it'll make me feel somewhat better.

My body is numb to the hot water as I slide into the tub. I close my eyes and try to relax, as I let the warm water consume me. I feel the grasp on mens hands as they start to massage my shoulders and it feels so good. Jake kisses along the side of my neck and whispers in my ear, *I love you.* I open my eyes and frantically look around. It was just a dream. The warm water is cold now so I rinse off and head back to my room. Getting over Jake is not going to be easy, especially if he is going to torment me in my dreams like that.

I have missed all last week of school and I'm sure I have some catching up to do. That's if my professors didn't drop me from my classes. I check my email and I have concerned emails from my professors, asking for an explanation. How do I explain what's happening in my life without sounding like a total nut case? I message them back and use the lame excuse of "emergency family problems" and tell them I will be back this upcoming week. Next I look over each syllabus to see what I missed and make a list of what I need to do catch up on. Luckily I was ahead in two of my classes so I only need to play catch up in two of my classes.

While reading my textbook that I lended to Jake previously, I come across a piece of paper at the end of the chapter. It's a poem.

Roses are red,
Violets are blue,
Would you be mad if I told you,
I love you?
-Jason

I become angry and tearful at the same time. Had this been in there this whole time? If I still didn't know Jason was Jake, this poem would have raised some suspicion. Goes to show Jake still has a thing for his cheesy poems. I let the anger take over and I crumble up the paper and toss it in the trash. As my anger subsides though, I hurry over to the trash can and take it out, trying to smooth out the paper. I use the paper to mark my place in the book, knowing full well I'm not going to be able to concentrate on reading after this. Simultaneously I get a text from Jake. *Can we talk?* I choose to ignore it and decide to finish checking my emails. I have an email from coach informing that I'm no longer a part of the team due to my irresponsible behavior and missing two practices and a game without any notice. I'm not shocked, but it still sucks. I was enjoying playing soccer again, but I can't expect no repercussions after disappearing for a week without a trace. I plop down on my bed and decide I better just go to sleep. I don't think I can handle any more disappointment today.

The next day I stay in bed until almost noon. I have no motivation to get out of bed, but I tell myself to not let my depression win once again. So, I force myself to get out of bed. I don't bother getting ready, I head downstairs in my pajamas and my hair still a mess. When I make it to then end of the stairs I hear my grandpa talking to a familiar voice. As I round the corner I see my grandpa and Thomas talking.

"What are you doing here?" I ask, interrupting their conversation. They both turn to me and Thomas makes his way over to me. "I just wanted to check on you. You weren't responding so I got worried again and thought I'd stop by to see if you were still here." As if I didn't already feel like a scum-bag enough, but to know he was afraid that I up and left him again made me feel like shit. "Oh. No, I just needed some time to myself so I turned my phone off." Which is true, after all the bad news yesterday I ended up shutting off my phone before I went to bed. "You look great" he says and I give him an exaggerated eye-roll. "It's true" Thomas says but then lowers his voice, "I mean if you want to change, I'd be willing to help" he adds. I immediately blush. "Do you mind if I steal Thomas from you grandpa?" "By all means, I need to get going anyway" my grandpa say. "Nice talking to you sir" Thomas says. "Please, call me Ralph" my grandpa replies as he shakes Thomas' hand.

Thomas follows me to the kitchen and offers to make me something to eat. I deny his offer as I pull out a bowl and pour myself some cereal. Thomas gives me a brief look of concern, but smartly decides against saying anything. "Did you have any plans today?" Thomas asks. "Does wallowing in self pity count?" Thomas opens his mouth to say something and once again changes his mind. "I'm not really sure how to feel about this whole situation either, but I'm trying here" Thomas says. "I know, I'm sorry. I am just trying to process everything. I've been on an emotional roller-coaster the past couple of days." Thomas comes around the counter and wraps his arms around me from behind. "I know, but it's not going to get any easier if you sit around and think about it all day. You need to start moving forward with your life." I turn around to see him and I re-study his face like I did the night of his party. I kiss him on the lips, convincing myself that I am capable of loving Thomas back. "You're right" I say when we break away.

I make my way back to my room after I promise Thomas that I'll call him later so we can make a movie date for tonight. Then the first thing I do is change since apparently it's frowned upon to be in pj's all day. Even though my heart still aches, being with Thomas helps dull that pain and it makes me look forward to going to the movies with him tonight. When I turn my phone back on, I have multiple missed calls from Jake, two missed calls from Thomas and a few texts from each. What gets my attention though is a text from a number that reads Blocked. I open the message and it says: *First comes love, then comes marriage, then comes a baby in a baby carriage…well, maybe not in that order… or with you.*

My blood begins to boil. Who does she think she is? As if it's not enough that she gets to have Jake, she has to taunt me about it too. I try calling Stacy's number, but she doesn't answer.

Chapter 8

Sunday flew by and now I am anxious to go back to school. I already know I'll see Jake in class and it has my nerves all over the place. Thomas offers to drive me to school and then walks me to class. I'm not sure if he's just being overly cautious or if it's his way of rubbing it in to Jake. As we are approach my class, Stacy is loitering outside of the room waiting for Jake I assume.

"See, I knew you'd move on quick" Stacy sneers. I am just about to call her an ugly name when Thomas speaks up, "Not as quick as it took you to get pregnant apparently." Stacy's jaw drops and I can't help but be astonished by his comeback as well. I look at Thomas and I have to resist the urge to kiss him right then and there. The fact Thomas has been so supportive and is standing by my side through this all says a lot and it makes me grow a little more attracted to him. Stacy shakes off her look of embarrassment and then gives me a devious smirk, "Oh look there's Jason." I don't know what irks me more, the fact she still calls him Jason or the fact that to her he is Jason. We both turn to see Jake approaching our now impromptu group. When I see him it takes everything I have not to run and jump into his arms and never let go.

Thomas and Jake just give each other a nod and then I meet Jake's gaze, I can see the hurt in his eyes. Stacy then makes her presence known as she loops her arm through Jake's and tugs on him. "Jason, I'm so glad you are here. I have been trying to get ahold of you because I need to ask you something important." Jake breaks his gaze from me and looks at Stacy, "I have an appointment today at four to check on the baby" she says as she rubs her belly. "Do you want to go with me?" Jake opens his mouth to say something, but the words don't come out and he gives me a bewildered look. I quickly turn away so no one can see the tears staring to well up.

Thomas puts his arm around me and ushers me away from them. "You don't need to be hearing this." "It's not like it's going to make it any less real" I say. "She's doing it on purpose and it's not right" Thomas says furiously. "I don't even want to go to class anymore" I tell him. "No, you're going. Don't give her the satisfaction of knowing she can get under your skin like that." He's right, I can't let Stacy think she can rule my life. "Alright, fine. Walk me back?" He grabs a hold of my hand and gives me a big smile. We make it back to the door of the classroom and I try to let go of Thomas' hand but he pulls me to him and plants a kiss on me. I should have broke away but I let the kiss linger for just a moment. As I pull away I give Thomas a bright smile, "See you later?" I ask him.

"Absolutely" he replies and then walks off. I turn to go into the classroom and I see Jake's tense body and clenched jaw and I could feel the heat of Stacy's eyes on me. "Pick me up later and I'll go with you" I hear Jake tell Stacy. I know it hurt him to witness what I just did but he needs to realize I'm doing it for his own good.

I try to sit next to some girl, but she informs me the seat is taken and I make my way back to my usual seat. Which means I'll have to sit next to Jake. It's not long before Jake plops down in the seat next to me and he turns to me. I try to pretend like I can't see him and keep my gaze on the whiteboard. "You're breaking my heart Sarah." I turn to him, "You think it isn't killing me too" I say. "Well it doesn't look that way." I shoot him a daggering look, "All I'm saying is, I get your upset with me, but this isn't fair. You know I love you and you're just going to kiss another guy in front of me, like my feelings don't matter?" I knew it wasn't right, but I was trying to get the point across. He needs to move on, I have. "I'm sorry, okay? I was hurt, especially after what your baby mama had just asked" I say bitterly. Jake rests his hand on top of mine, "I would give anything for it to be you" Jake tells me. I don't know how to respond and luckily I don't have to, because the professor enters the room and starts talking. Just in time too, I don't think I could've handled another second of his touch and pleading gaze.

When class finishes I hurry and gather up my things and flee the classroom. "Sarah" Jake calls out, but I keep walking, telling myself to ignore him. He catches up to me and cuts me off. "What Jake?" "Just tell me that it wasn't all a lie. Tell me you still love me like the way I love you." I start to cry and it attracts strange looks from the people passing by. Jake embraces me and I half heartedly push him away and punch him the chest. "You idiot. Why do I have to say anything? The whole reason I'm doing this is because I love you. Don't you see that?" Jake steps back and wipes the tears from my eyes with his thumb. I gaze into his eyes once again and I'm trapped, I can't look away and I knew what was coming next and I didn't even stop it. Jake kisses me and I could feel the passion surge through my entire body. I don't think anyone can make me feel the way I do when I kiss Jake. We can't keep doing this I tell myself. I pull away, "Jake stop" I say sternly, "I have a boyfriend." I can tell my words cut deep as he lets go of me, "You're right, and I have a pregnant girlfriend" he says and walks off. As I watch him walk away, it feels as if each step sends a stab to my heart. I want to chase after him and tell him it was all just an act, that I don't care as long as I get to be with him, but I stay right where I am and watch him fade into the distance.

I decide to skip getting lunch and sit on a bench to listen to music till my next class. Part of me wonders if I should go back to Kentucky after I finish the semester. I'll have my degree and at that point I can start fresh. I imagine running into Ms. Henson and how smug she'll be, knowing she essentially got what she always wanted and I decide that going back to Kentucky wouldn't be a good idea. Maybe I'll go somewhere new, away from everyone and start fresh.

It's almost three when I get out of my last class and all I can think about is the fact that Jake is probably getting ready for the appointment with Stacy. I can't imagine being a young mom. Jake has always wanted to be a dad, even though I'd be happy just having him to myself. I just wish I could have been the one to fulfill that dream. I guess that's what I get for being selfish. Thomas taps me on the shoulder and interrupts my gloomy daydreaming. "Hey babe" "Hi" I reply. "Did you want to go the gym or do you wanna go back home and chill?" "Let's go do some cardio, I think it'll help." "Good idea" he says.

After putting in some miles on the elliptical, my endorphins kick in and my heightened emotions overtake me. I approach Thomas as he's lifting weights and he turns to greet me. "Done already?" He asks. "Not quite" I say, giving him a wink. "Follow me" I mouth to him. He sets down the weights and I lead him to the locker rooms. "Do you want me to go change?" He asks. "I want you to go in and tell me if anyone's in there" I tell him. "Okay" he says slowly and then turns to go in the locker room. He disappears for a moment and then remerges from the locker room. "No, is there supposed to be?" "Us" I say as

I quickly pull him into the men's locker room and lead him to the showers.

Thomas catches on to my intentions and turns on the hot water and starts to undress me while I take his clothes off. I press my sweaty body to his as he smothers me with kisses. We let the water engulf us as I kiss him back and let our hands roam each others bodies. I have never been with anyone other than Jake and I feel like a traitor, but it is such a thrill at the same time. Thomas runs his hands further and further down my body and I become limp. He picks me up and I wrap my legs around his waist as his body overtakes mine. I am captivated by how gentle yet equally overpowering Thomas is as he consumes me and overwhelms all of my sensations.

"I love you" Thomas says as he releases me from his grasp and gives me one last kiss. I stare into his eyes and realize that I may not love him, yet, but I love the way he makes me feel and I think my mind got the two confused because I speak without thinking. "I love you too" I feel myself say. A huge smile spreads across his face. Why did I say that? I'm letting my emotions get the best of me. It's not like the potential to love Thomas isn't there. I just feel bad for letting him think we are on the same level in our relationship. It's not like I can take it back though. "You are absolutely amazing. I don't even know how to describe how wonderful that was" Thomas says. If my cheeks aren't already red from the shower, he could see me blushing.

We both get redressed and Thomas helps sneak me out of the locker room. "See you in a minute" I tell him as I go to get my things from the women's locker room. Thomas holds my hand as we walk to his car and I can't help but notice how happy he is.

Thomas is having a hard time leaving me after spending the rest of the afternoon with me at my grandparents and I'm not sure if it's because we took our relationship to the next level or the fact I told him I love him. It could be both, who knows. I can't lie, being with Thomas intimately does make me feel closer to him and it makes me eager for our next encounter. I am still shocked that I had the courage to do what we did, but endorphins can be a powerful thing. I know what we did was a dangerous game to play. The pull out method is not an effective form of birth control and it reminds me that I need to go see a gynecologist now that I am being sexually active again.

After Thomas leaves, I lay on my bed and just waste my time staring at the ceiling. I'm not really sure how to feel about everything. I probably didn't make the smartest decisions today, but it is what it is. I shouldn't feel guilty for having sex with Thomas. After all, Jake had sex with Stacy, so now we have both been with other people. With time, Jake will realize what I've done for him and then maybe we can at least be friends. Who am I kidding? Me and Jake could never be, *just* friends. That's why I've decided after this semester is over, I am moving away. I haven't decided where, maybe Texas or New York or Seattle. Thinking about Texas reminds me of Blake and I wonder whatever happened to him. Not sure if he would be disappointed or relieved that things didn't work out between me and Jake. I think about texting him to see how he's doing, but I decide it's better to not willingly invite unnecessary chaos back into my life.

Chapter 9

The next day in between classes, I call my manager Beth to see if she will still let me work at Frozen Swirls. I knew she would agree since they are desperate for help, especially since Stacy up and quit and so did Blake. It doesn't surprise me that Blake quit, the only reason he took the job was to keep an eye on me and try to lure me from Jake. But for Stacy to quit, that was a bit shocking. I guess that means I'll be lead team member, and, since I got kicked off the soccer team, I'll be available to work my life away. Beth insinuates that the sooner I can come back the better, so I tell her I'll be there after class and it makes her ecstatic.

As much as I don't want to go to work, it'll be good for me. Hopefully it'll distract me from everything that's going on. When I arrive Beth is eager to give me my new name tag that distinguishes me as team lead and inform me of my 50 cent raise for my promotion. Normally I would be excited, but for one, I got promoted by default, and two, how can I be a team lead when there is no team to lead? Oh well, I need to get over my pride and just be grateful I still have my job. After all, I've pretty much lost everything else.

By time work is over I am exhausted, but I promised Thomas I would go to his game. When I show up I instantly regret my decision. It slipped my mind that Stacy is the girls team manager and it looks like Jake showed up to support her. I quickly find Thomas and make my way to him. "Hey babe, glad you made it. We were just about to go to the locker room and change" Thomas tells me. "Okay. Would you be mad if I didn't stay the whole time? Work wore me out today." "Not at all. I'm just glad I got to see your beautiful face" he replies with a smile and gives me a kiss before he heads to the locker room. I go and take a seat in the bleachers and soon after I sit down I get a text from Jake.

Jake: *I'm sorry.* I glance to where he is sitting and our eyes lock for a quick second before I turn away. I reply: *For what?* Jake: *I showed up to watch you play and I think Stacy knew it because she told me you were kicked off the team.* Despite the odds we are at he still showed up to support me and it gives my heart a warm fuzzy feeling and then I have to remind myself that it doesn't matter anymore. I text him back: *It doesn't matter, it's my own fault.* Jake replies: *Can we please talk? Meet me at the concession stand.* I know I shouldn't, but I can't say no. I see Jake stand up and make his way down the bleachers and it's as if my body is on auto-pilot because I stand up and make my way down too.

I shove my way through the crowd and I can see Jake standing by one of the support beams. I'm almost to him when I hear a man's voice shout "Jason!" I direct my gaze past Jake and see a middle-aged man with a flushed face quickly approaching Jake. I stop where I'm at to observe the interaction between Jake and this mystery man. Jake turns to face the guy and the man stops a couple inches from Jake's face and begins to yell at him. "You got my daughter pregnant and now you're going to pay" the man who I can only assume to be Stacy's father says. Jake starts to stutter from the angry confrontation, "I, I, I am sorry sir" is all he manages to say. The man pokes Jake's chest forcefully, "Oh we are way past sorry, you son of a bitch. You better do the right thing if you know what's good for you." "Sir I've already told Stacy I would be there every step of the way" Jake tells the man. "Damn right you will and you're going to marry her in hopes of redeeming any self-worth you two once had. And if you tell her about this encounter, you're going to wish you didn't" the man says and then stomps off.

Me and Jake make eye contact from across the way and I can't find the will to go over to him. Jake begins to walk towards me and I take off in the opposite direction. I didn't want to hear what he had to say anymore because it doesn't matter. It doesn't matter how much he loves me or wants to be with me because, this encounter with Stacy's dad gave me a dose of reality. Any figment of hope that things could actually work between us was just erased. I knew this is where things would lead eventually, I just didn't think it would be so soon. I don't go back to watch the game I just go to my car and leave.

For the first time in awhile, I feel completely shattered. I mean is drama just drawn to me? It's hard to picture a time in my life when times were good, especially when those times seem so far away. I stop by the liquor store on my way home and buy a bottle of vodka with every intention of drowning my sorrows when I get home. When I make it home, I smuggle the vodka up to my room. I mean it's not like I'm underage, I just don't want my grandparents to know what I'm doing.

The next hour I spend laying in my pajamas drinking straight from the bottle. My liver is going to hate me one day. I wish there were healthier self-destructing options, but I guess that defeats the whole purpose of self-destruction. A soft knock at my door sends me jolting up, I frantically try to find a place to stuff the bottle of vodka while simultaneously asking "Who is it?"

"It's Jake." I freeze in my tracks and then slowly make my way to the door. I open my door and greet him with a scowl. "What are you doing here?" I hiss. He glances at the bottle in my hand and snatches it from me. "Hey give that back" I say as I try to grab the bottle from him. I am unsteady on my feet and I fall into him. "You don't need to be doing this to yourself" he tells me. "Why not? It's none of your business what I do anymore." He steps into my room and plops down on my bed. "Um excuse me, what are you doing?" I ask, but Jake doesn't say anything. He takes the lid off the bottle and takes a large swig of it without even a grimace. As I study him he begins to chuckle. "What's so funny?" I ask. "Nothing. I'm just delirious. I haven't slept good in days, I've hardly ate, and it seems like every corner I turn I find myself in a bigger mess than I was before." I walk over to my bed and sit next to him. "Ditto" I say as I take the bottle from him and take a sip myself. "I don't want to marry her Sarah. I want to marry you" he tells me. "I know, but you have to you, you need to. It's the right thing to do and that's why I broke it off." "I know and that's why I want you to know, I will always love you" Jake says and then stands up. He gives me one more good look and then turns to leave. I grab his hand, "Wait" I say. He looks at me and I know he can see the conflicting emotions all over my face. "Stay" I whisper. "Sarah, you're drunk." "Just because I'm drunk doesn't mean I love you any less" I tell him before continuing, "Do you really want to go though the rest of our lives thinking, I wish?" I tell him. Jake does't need anymore convincing as his lips collide with mine, causing a rush of adrenaline to take over my body.

Jake picks me up and sits me in the center of my bed and climbs on top of me. We both hesitate for a split second as we stare into each others eyes, but it only causes more tension. We start to fumble our clothes as we strip each other down. Jake kisses me passionately and it only makes my body yearn for him even more, but Jake takes his time. He teases me with his wandering hands, until I can't take it any more, "Jake please" I beg. "Open your eyes" he whispers in my ear. I open my eyes and I see Jake staring down at me, he doesn't break his gaze as our bodies connect. I let out a groan and it encourages Jake to keep going. We continue to please one another for the next half hour. When we finish we collapse onto the bed, intertwined together, Jake looks at me and tells me "I love you." "I love you too" I reply as I lay my head on his chest.

I know I am going to regret this decision when the realization that I'll never get to be with Jake again settles in. It shouldn't be a competition, but my time with Thomas was nothing compared to tonight. It must be true what they say, break-up sex is some of the best. Jake always had a way of leaving me satisfied, but tonight was invigorating. It has been so long and I didn't think I'd ever get to feel this way again and I can't help but let the thoughts overwhelm me. Jake holds me as I cry myself to sleep.

The next morning, I wake up feeling refreshed, despite my pounding headache. If Jake wasn't still fast asleep next to me I would've thought last night was just a dream. I lay there admiring his handsome physique and remembering the night we shared. Jake wakes up and sees me staring at him. "Good morning" he tells me while giving me his gorgeous smile. Even though I know once he leaves things will be over between us, I'm determined to savor this moment as long as I can. "Good morning" I reply as I run my fingers through his hair. "I wish I could wake up like this every morning" Jake says. "Me too" I say glumly. Jake rolls over and looks at the clock. "Oh shit" Jake says as he jumps out of bed and starts to get dressed. "Leaving so soon?" I ask. Jake stops and lets out a sigh, " I was supposed to be at work an hour ago and with everything going on, I really need this job." "Oh" I say, trying to hide my disappointment. Jake finishes getting ready then kneels in front of me and takes my hands in his. "Sarah Caldwell, I love you and I will never stop loving you. There will never be a day when you walk into the room and you don't take my breath away. You'll always be the one" Jake says and then gives me one long kiss.

When I open my eyes he is gone and I don't hold it in anymore. I break down and cry. My heart feels entirely crushed and I want nothing more than to go on a full rampage. I want to break something, punch something, scream at the top of my lungs, just anything to release the frustration and heart break I feel right now. For the first time ever I actually wish I could go to school, but today is the first day of fall break and now I have nothing to do, but lay around and think about my stupid feelings. If I didn't think life was cruel before I found out Jake was alive, I definitely think it is now. Part of me wishes that I still thought he was dead, but it doesn't matter. I had fallen for Jake all over again when I knew him as Jason. I didn't even know it was possible to fall in love with the same person twice. Life sure is twisted.

Chapter 10

As the next few weeks pass, life just slips into a mundane routine. If I'm not at school then I'm at work. Me and Thomas have been hanging out almost every other day and things are going well for us. However, we have agreed to hold off on anymore sex until I can go see a doctor and get on some birth control. With how smooth things have been going between us, Thomas has thrown out the idea of moving in together, but I am leery about the idea. For one, I don't know if I'm ready for that type of commitment yet. Secondly, I have not told him my intentions of moving away at the end of the semester. If I do move away, that will be a headache for everyone involved. Should I even continue to date Thomas if I plan on moving away to start fresh? Maybe he will want to come with and we can start our life together? It would be nice to get out of my grandparents, but I don't think that's enough of an excuse to rush into living with my boyfriend.

Today is my first off day since I started working again and it is long overdue. I want more than anything just to sit back and relax, but I have to actually be an adult and make some phone calls and get an oil change. I get myself an appointment set up two weeks from now with a doctor who also specializes in women's health, that way I can kill two birds with one stone. Once I get done making my appointment and working out some errors with financial aid I get ready and take my car to get an oil change. On the way back from the dealership I give my mom a call and tell her that I need her to get in contact with our hospital in Kentucky to send over my information to the office I'll be going to. I can't believe I'm going to go through all this hassle again in a couple months when I move away from California. Although the thought of being on my own is exhilarating, it makes me equally nervous thinking about being a young woman out on my own. Who would protect me? I try to brush off the negative thoughts and think about how good the move will be for me.

When I get back to the house I do some homework and work on a paper that is due next week. After two grueling hours of research for my paper I take a break to pant my nails. I haven't been able to paint my nails in a long time and it felt good to pamper myself. Now if only I could refrain from biting them so they can stay decent looking. Another hour passes and Thomas asks if he can come over now that practice is over. On the way over, Thomas stops to get a movie and when he arrives I make us some popcorn. I enjoy our impromptu stay at home date nights.

I feel like I've done a good job of steering clear of Jake. During class we speak the bare minimum to each other and keep it strictly school related. Stacy must be pleased with herself because she has Jake practically conjoined at her hip. It's as if I never existed in either of their lives, but I guess that was the plan all along. I'm dreading the day Stacy shows up with a ring on her finger. So far Jake hasn't proposed, despite what Stacy's dad demanded. I can only hope that he waits till the end of the semester so I won't have to face him in class, or face either one of them at that. Knowing Stacy, she will try to rub it in and I don't think I will be able to hide how it'll effect me. Surely, he won't use my ring, or the ring he used to propose to me with, I should say. I need to quit thinking about him, I tell myself. I've done okay, but it's times like this when I have too much free time to think that it gets the best of me. Even when I have a successful day of not thinking of him, he visits me in my dreams, which is worse because I can't escape from him.

The next morning I wake up and debate if I should show up late to class or even go at all. Today is Monday and it's the class Jake and I share. Stacy makes it an annoying point to walk him to class and I'm not sure if it's her own obsessive reason for doing so or if she's trying to stick it to me. Either way it makes me dread going to class. I suck it up and tell myself I only have two more months and then it'll all be over. I'm still trying to decide on where I should move to, but I figure it'll be somewhere that I can put my degree to use.

When I make it to class I take my usual seat and pull out my book to get ahead on some reading. It's not long before Stacy and Jake come along, right on cue. I can't help but notice that Stacy is finally starting to show and it makes me feel especially bitter today when they kiss and part ways. I instantly regret at least not showing up late today. Jake takes his seat next me and part of me wants to ask him all the gritty details. How far a long is she? Do they know the gender yet? I refrain from doing so, realizing that it'll make no difference if I know. Besides, I couldn't give him the impression that I care or seem like I'm jealous. For some reason, seeing Stacy with her slight baby bump, makes it hard for me to sit next to Jake, let alone focus in class. Probably because the realization has settled in. That's why when the professor dismisses class I quickly gather my things and try to hurry out of the room, but, being the klutz I am, I trip over my chair and drop my things. Jake rushes to my side to check on me and once I establish that I am physically okay just stunned with embarrassment, he helps me pick up my things. Jake picks up my book and out falls the makeshift bookmark, which also happens to be the poem he had written me. He picks it up and gives me a heart-aching look. I snatch it from him and leave the room. How could I have been so careless? Why did I leave that in there?

Work is going smoothly until I get ready to close. As I'm putting away the extra buckets of frozen yogurt I hear the door chime and make my way back to the floor. Before I round the corner I can see it's Jake and I freeze in my tracks. Luckily he's distracted by looking at the flavors and hasn't noticed me yet. I do my best to resume my composure and come around the corner with my best game face on. "Welcome to Frozen Swirls, what can I get you?" Jake looks up and I can tell my presence catches him off guard. "Sarah, um, sorry. I didn't think you still worked here" Jake says. "Yep, sure do" I reply awkwardly. We both stand there in silence until Jake clears his throat and points towards the cups. "Right" I say with a nervous laugh, "what size would you like?" "A medium." I hand him the medium sized cup and watch him make his way over to the machines and I try to distract myself so I'm not gawking at him the entire time. He makes his way back over to the bar. "Would you like any toppings?" I ask. "No, I don't think she wants any" Jake says in a remorseful tone. I take a hard swallow at the revelation that he is getting Stacy some frozen yogurt. I should've known though, Jake doesn't like mint chocolate. I give him a nod and ring up his order. Jake turns to go but then swiftly turns back to me and tries to meet my gaze. I look away and focus my attention on the register as if it's the most fascinating contraption I ever laid my eyes on. "Sarah" Jake says. "Thanks for stopping in, but we are actually closing so you'll have to come back another time" I say in my best customer service voice. Jake knows I don't want to hear what he has to say so he closes his mouth and simply walks out.

Two interactions with Jake in one day, sheesh. I feel like I need a drink or a nice long bubble bath. When I make it home I choose the latter of the two options. I'm so frustrated with myself. I knew I should've left that poem in the trash. Now he probably thinks I'm still all strung up on him. Who am I kidding? I am still strung on Jake. It's going to take more than just a couple weeks for me to get over him. He is and always will be, the love of my life. When I finish my bath, I return to my room and check my phone. I missed a call from Haley so I decide to call her back to help distract me.

By time I get off the phone, I am searching for entry level executive assistant jobs. Haley has convinced me the sooner I start looking, the easier it'll be to make it a reality. After I graduate, I should be able to get a job as an executive assistant, that's my dream job anyway. There are quite a few listings in New York of course, but I don't know if I could handle living in New York on my own. I keep browsing and there are some postings in South Carolina, Maine, Oklahoma, Texas, and Georgia. There are way more options for smaller businesses, these are just the ones for some big time corporations. At least now I know I have my options open. Atlanta wouldn't be too bad of an idea. I'll be close to home, but still far enough away to be on my own. I try to remind myself not to get set on one place and save the postings so I can apply later.

The next morning as I'm making myself some coffee I get a text. Jake: *Are you sure there's no way we can be together?* Good to know yesterday's interactions didn't just stir up my feelings. I reply: *I'm sorry, but yes I am sure.* I can tell Jake goes back and forth on his reply as I see his message bubble disappear and reappear multiple times. After a couple minutes he replies: *Then I have no choice, I can't put it off any longer.* Even though I am a thousand percent sure I know he's talking about proposing to Stacy, I can't help but be in denial. As disappointed and crushed I am, the psycho ex in me wants to inquire on his plans. How is he going to do it? Will it be intimate? Will it be in public so everyone can share in their special moment? I suddenly feel jealous because Jake never got to actually propose to me in such a way. I guess he doesn't need to ask for her dad's blessing since he's the whole reason Jake is doing this in the first place. I try to brush off my obsessive thoughts and get ready for school.

I notice as I go about my day, I can't help but feel on edge. I've already snapped at Thomas twice and I have been mean mugging the entire school. I feel like I owe Thomas an explanation, but then that means I would have to tell him the whole reason I am upset is because I basically gave Jake the approval to propose to Stacy. It's all I can think about. Instead I apologize and tell him it's that time of the month and redeem myself by making plans for us to hang out later. Thomas gives me a passionate kiss, letting me know all is forgiven and then heads to class. I make my way to the library and on my way there, I am caught off guard by Stacy and Jake holding hands, making their way to the library too. We make it to the door at the same and Stacy greets me with a sneer as I hold open the door. My eyes quickly dart to her left hand, searching for a ring, but I don't see one, which means he hasn't done it yet. I think Jake knew what I was doing because when I look at him he turns his gaze to the ground. "You're welcome" I say, playing it off as Stacy walks through the door without telling me thank you. I see her roll her eyes and keep walking. We part our ways once in the library and I tell myself repeatedly not to look back, but my will is not that strong today. I look over my shoulder and my eyes meet with Jake. The look we give each other could probably ignite a fire with the spark we share, but it's as if there are two magnets at each end of the library, pulling us further and further apart. I'd give anything to feel his embrace just once more. Stop it, I tell myself. I can't think like that, he's going to be engaged. I have to let him move on with his life.

Chapter 11

I skip the next two days of school and just pick up extra hours at work. I don't want to see Stacy's smug face as she flaunts around with her newly engaged vibe. I want to give it a couple days and hopefully let the news settle. Who knows, maybe he didn't even plan on doing it till this weekend and I missed school for no reason. Oh well, the less I have to be around them, the better.

When Saturday rolls around, Beth agrees to let me take an extended lunch so I can go watch Thomas's game. I would think that is extremely nice of her, but I've overheard her talking to the owner about how much overtime I'm getting. It's not like we necessarily have a line out the door begging for applications. It would be nice to share the work load some though. I thought I could handle working so much, but it's getting exhausting.

I decide to show up late to the game for two reasons. One, so I'm not gone that long and two, to avoid Stacy. Fortunately, I arrive just as the girls team is leaving the field and I am able to watch the game in peace. The guys end up winning and celebrate with a refreshing Gatorade shower. I never understood the concept of doing that. All I can think about is how sticky I would feel after it dries. That's why when Thomas approaches me for a hug I opt to give him a kiss instead. Once Thomas leaves for the locker room I make my way back to work.

When I make it back to work, I take over for Beth, but she stays and helps me settle the afternoon rush. Then, just as Beth is about to leave, Stacy walks in. I can tell Jake didn't tell her I still worked here, because Stacy is taken aback when she sees me, but quickly hides her shock and resumes her typical snobby demeanor. "Good, I'm so glad you're both here" Stacy says. "What can we do for you Stacy?" Beth asks. "Well I just felt terrible the way I left you in a bind so I thought I'd make an offer to help bring in some revenue for the business." I can tell Stacy has peaked Beth's interest. "What did you have in mind?" Beth asks her. Stacy looks at me and gives me a hateful smile before turning back to Beth. "Well in case you haven't heard the news, I am now engaged" Stacy says as she flaunts the ring to me and Beth. I suddenly feel hot and queasy. Stay cool, I tell myself. "How wonderful, congratulations!" Beth tells her excitedly. Stacy looks at me and I remain silent. "Thank you" Stacy says before continuing, "Anyways, I was thinking, what if I had my engagement party here?" I can't control my emotions any longer, as my mouth falls open and I reply, "You've got to be joking?" Beth looks at me and then back at Stacy. "I'm sorry you don't think it's a good idea Sarah, but it's not your decision, it's Beth's" Stacy tells me and then turns to Beth, giving her the most flattering smile she has. Beth doesn't know what has happened between us and must be confused. I know she is weighing the options and the party would be good for business, especially since the store was closed for a week due to our whole escapade. "That is a very kind offer and I would be delighted to host your engagement party here. Are you sure you want to celebrate your special day here though?" Beth asks as she gestures to the building as if it's not an elaborate enough place to throw the party. Stacy looks at me once more and gives a devious smirk before responding, "Oh, I'm positive."

Stacy and Beth go in the back to go over details and finalize the arrangements. I am glad there aren't any customers because, I am so pissed off I don't think I could muster up any fake customer service mannerisms right now. Surely Jake won't let this happen. I wonder if he's told his mom yet and if she will be at the party. That would just make her day, to see me catering Jake's engagement to another woman. Maybe I can have Jake talk Stacy out of it, but after seeing Stacy's vengeful look, I doubt it'll do any good except make the matter worse.

"Great, thanks so much Beth" Stacy says as she emerges from the office. Stacy walks past me as she flips her hair and gives me her devious smirk. "See you around" she says and then leaves. Beth comes out of her office a few moments later and goes to leave, but stops and turns to me. "Did I miss something between you two? I thought you were friends" Beth says. I give a large huff, I might as well tell her so she can cut me some slack. "She's engaged to my ex-fiance. She practically black-mailed him into being with her after he got her pregnant." If I wasn't in such a bad mood, the look on Beth's face could have made me bust out in laughter. My response, leaves Beth in shock and she tries to hide her look of remorse. "Um, I'm sorry Sarah. I wish I would've known. Unfortunately, we really need this money or I would tell her never mind." "No it's okay, I understand" I tell her. "I really hate to put you in this awkward position, but if it'll make it easier on you I can come in and help out the day of the party" Beth tells me. "You would do that?" I ask. "Of course. Besides, that would be too much for one person to handle on their own" she tells me. "Thanks Beth I really appreciate that" I reply. "Just so you know the party is next Thursday, but I told her she could stop by to make payments and go over details. I will tell her to handle all arrangements through me though. That way there isn't any awkward tension between you two." "Okay, thanks" I tell her. Beth finally leaves, which leaves me on my own, at last. Since there still aren't any customers I go to the bathroom and take a moment to gather myself.

I hear the door chime so I pull myself together and make my way back on the floor. Jake sees me and runs over to me and engulfs me in a big hug. I push him away, paranoid that someone might see. "What are you doing?" I ask. "Stacy just stopped by and told me that she booked Frozen Swirls for our engagement party." "Yep, she sure did" I reply. "Sarah, I am so sorry. I tried to convince her to change her mind, but she's pretty set on the idea." "It doesn't surprise me. Talk about the ultimate middle finger to me." "Can you at least look at me?" Jake pleads. I reluctantly draw my gaze up to his eyes and I can see the flicker of sorrow in his eyes. I raise my hand up and cup the side of his face in my hand and then pull it away. "Congratulations" I tell him. The door chimes once more, indicating that I finally have a customer. "I need to get back to work" I tell him. He gives me a nod and disappears while I direct my attention on the customer.

Even though me and Thomas have a date tonight, I am looking forward to today being over with. By time I get off work I am mentally exhausted, but I put on my best poker face and greet Thomas with a smile when I show up to his house to change. I've actually been looking forward to this date. There's a new arcade that has a bunch of classic and retro games, along with some pool tables and a fifties diner-esque eating area that we are going to tonight. I wish I was in a better state of mind, but I try to make the best of it anyway.

Our date ends up being a perfect ending to a horrible day. I didn't want to ruin it by telling him the news, I figured that could wait till tomorrow. Maybe Beth would let Thomas come help at the party so I can have his support. As I am about to leave for the night Thomas pulls me into a long kiss. "Thanks for tonight" he tells me. "I should be thanking you" I reply giving him another short kiss "So, when is your appointment again? I don't think I can keep my hands off you much longer" Thomas tells me. I blush and I can feel my face getting hot, "um Wednesday" I tell him. It's flattering to know he's still crazy about me. I admit, I had my doubts after we had sex. I was curious if he was only sticking around until I finally gave it up, but if anything it's made him head over heels for me. Maybe this means he really is in it for the long run? The guilt overwhelms me and I decide that it's not fair for me to keep secrets from him. Last time it turned out terribly, so I tell myself I need to tell him about planning to move away.

"Thomas, I have something to tell you." "What is it?" He asks nervously. "Since things are getting serious between us, I just wanted to let you know that at the end of semester, when I graduate, I was thinking about moving." Thomas' demeanor becomes serious. "What, why?" He asks. "There's a bunch of job openings for the position I want. If I stay here it'll be too cut throat." Thomas remains silent. "Please say something, I thought you'd be happy for me." "Does this have anything to do with getting away from Jake?" He asks me. He's a smart guy, I'll give him that. "Some of it, it'll be easier to move on if his presence isn't rubbed in my face everyday" I reply. "What does this mean for us?" He asks me. I look at him and I can see he's trying not to get emotional. I grab his hand and give it a squeeze, "Remember what you told me? If you're willing to make this work then I am." He gives me a pitiful smile. "I just hate that I don't graduate till May, otherwise I'd go with you." "You would?" I ask, slightly shocked. "I'd do anything for you" he tells me. I give him an excited kiss. He laughs, "I take it that's the response you were looking for" he says. "Your support means everything to me" I say. "Do you know where you're going yet?" He asks me. I shake my head, "Not officially, but I was leaning towards Atlanta." He nods his head from side to side as if he's weighing the pros and cons. "That's not as bad as it could be" he finally says. I flash him a smile and he kisses my forehead. When we finish discussing my future plan we exchange our good-byes and I leave.

The next few days go by way too quickly and now it's Wednesday, the day of my appointment. Not going to lie, I am a little nervous and I don't know why. I mean I don't think anyone necessarily likes a stranger messing with their private parts, but that's the price we have to pay I guess. I don't see guys having to go through this type of embarrassment. I quit my complaining and get ready for my appointment. I plan to leave earlier than usual since it's my first appointment and I need to fill out paperwork.

By time I make it to the office, I am thirty minutes early and I make my way in. I take a seat and start to fill out all the applicable paper work. After fifteen minutes I finally turn in the papers. "Thank you Ms. Caldwell. The doctor will review the papers and your files that were sent over and we will get you in a room to be seen." "Thanks" I say and then return to my seat. Another fifteen minutes pass before they call me to a room and ask me to change into a gown. I am anxiously awaiting for the doctor to come in and I am relieved when I see a woman enter the room. The website didn't say whether the doctors were a female or not, so it made choosing who to see nerve-wrecking.

"Hi there, I am Dr. Hampton. I'll be the one taking over your care" she says with a pleasant smile. "Hi" I reply sheepishly. "Please don't be nervous. I want you to feel comfortable opening up to me" she says. Good one, I think to myself. "Lets start with you telling me what's bringing you in today? Is anything bothering you at the moment?" She asks. "Not quite. I just want to get on some birth control since I have become sexually active again and with a new partner." "Alright, we can manage that. Are you sure your new partner has been practicing safe sex with his prior partners or would you like to be checked for any sexually transmitted diseases as well?" I had not even thought about it in that aspect, but given Thomas's reputation in the past, I oblige to her suggestion. "Very well, we can get that done when we move onto the physical exam." I give her a nod showing my approval. "Well it's reassuring to know that you have not let your miscarriage keep you from having a healthy sex life. Sometimes after a miscarriage, women struggle with intimacy after the fact." I let out a small laugh, "I'm sorry, but I believe you have me confused with another patient" I tell her. She grabs the folder from the counter and looks at it for a moment. "You are Sarah Caldwell is that correct?" "Um, yes, but I have never been pregnant" I tell her. She glances through a couple papers and then clears her throat, "Ms. Caldwell, I have a dictation here from an ER doctor in Kentucky who states he took care of you when you were in a bad car accident. You suffered from, all things considering, some minor injuries aside from the large gash that runs from your left hip down to your left thigh. They thought that your gash was where all the bleeding was coming from, but once they got it controlled they noticed the bleeding was coming from elsewhere and that's when they discovered you were miscarrying. It says here, the doctor notified, a woman at your bedside who claimed to be your mother and told him she would inform you when you came through." It's as if I am in a war zone, because as the words roll out of her mouth I become shell-shocked. Her voice fades in the distance and I start to hyperventilate as I clench my abdomen with both hands. "Sarah, stay with me" I hear Dr. Hampton shout. She lays me back and gets a cold wash cloth to place on my forehead. Surely my own mother wouldn't keep such a big secret from me? Had I really been pregnant and not known it? I wasn't the best about remembering to take my birth control and me and Jake couldn't keep our hands off one another so the possibility is there. My first instinct is to tell him, but what good will it do? It will only make the history we share that much more intense. "How far along was I?" Dr. Hampton gives me a concerned look, "You mean to tell me you did not know you were pregnant?" I shake my head. "I am so sorry to spring this on you" she tells me first before continuing, "according to the doctors notes, you had to be approximately 12-14 weeks along." I start to cry and Dr. Hampton hands me some tissues. "If you want, we can post-pone the rest of your appointment for another day?" She tells me compassionately. I blow my nose and shake my head once more, "No, it's okay. I want to get this over with" I tell her and she gives me an understanding nod.

When I finish my appointment, I hurry to my car and have another cry session. My sadness quickly subsides and it is replaced with anger. I pull out my phone and dial my moms number. "How could you?" I yell when she answers the phone. "Excuse me?" She retorts. "The night of my accident, the doctor told you I had miscarried and you didn't even tell me" I shout in between sobs. "Sarah, what on earth are you talking about? I had no idea. I never spoke with any of your doctors that night" she tells me. I can hear her asking for more details, but I zone out when I realize who it was. Ms. Henson, that sly conniving bitch. I should have known this had her name written all over it. That's why she faked his death. She panicked at how close we almost came to being connected forever, which is exactly what she didn't want. "I'll call you back" I say flatly before hanging up on my mom.

Chapter 12

I had told myself I wasn't going to tell Jake about my discovery, but he deserves to know why his mom did what she did. I am not far from his place so I decide to head straight to his apartment so I can tell him in person. When I make it to his place, I rush up the stairs and knock on the door. I have no idea how he is going react. What are the odds that we almost had a kid together and now he's actually going to have a kid with Stacy? I hear a woman giggling on the other side of the door and then finally the door opens and I see Stacy in a robe with wet hair. I am stunned at what I see. "What do you want?" Stacy snaps. "I came to talk to Jake, I have to tell him something very important" I say. "Well if you can't tell we are in the middle of an early afternoon rendezvous." "Shut it Stacy, this is serious." "He's quite the lover ya know" she says seductively. I ignore her, "Jake" I shout, hoping to get his attention. "He's in the shower, he can't hear you" she says and then shuts the door in my face.

As if I wasn't furious enough as it is. Now I got to see first hand how close they actually are. I feel disgusting and now I want to go home and take a shower myself. I make my way back to my car and I can't believe who I see unloading luggage from their car. "Mary" I say sternly. Ms. Henson whips around to face me, "Sarah, I would say it's a surprise to see you, but I'm sure you are here begging Jake to take you back" she tells me. The nerve of this woman, I let out a scoff. "No, actually, I was stopping by because I found something out today that I felt like he should know" I say giving her a smirk. "And what's that?" She inquires. "How his mommy dearest forgot to tell us that I miscarried our baby the night of our accident." Ms. Henson quickly shuts her trunk and tries to escape my wrath, but I knock her bag out of her hand and block her from taking another step. "Where do you think you're going?" I say, "we aren't finished here." "I have nothing to say to you" she hisses. "That seems to be the common theme with you. You don't like to tell me anything" I tell her. "Does it matter? You are his past and Stacy is his future." "Yeah, all because of you. You couldn't handle the fact we were happy together because you are scared of being all alone. You are just a bitter, hateful woman" I shout. I can see the tears start to form in her eyes, but she quickly wipes them away. "You're wrong. You are just a conceited snobby little brat who is, and never will be good enough for Jake. You thought you were so cool, drinking al the time and being careless. You say you love Jake, but all the stupid things you involved him could have gotten his scholarship taken away. You didn't care about him, you just cared that he made you look good and made you popular." She knew how to push every single one of my buttons. "So what's the damage now? I'm sure he's on the verge of breaking off his engagement with that poor girl, now that you've selfishly told him your news. Did you mention that you were an alcoholic and the baby didn't have a chance anyway?" My fight or flight senses kick in and I smack her. She grabs her cheek and looks at me appalled. "For your information, I didn't tell him. I couldn't bring myself to do it when Stacy answered the door" I tell her and then walk off. The last part may have been a lie, but I had to make it seem like I had the slightest bit of integrity.

I make it back to my car and I break down in tears. I don't know how I'm going to make it through tomorrow. Between Ms. Henson and Stacy, they are ruthless and they are going to rip me to shreds. I immediately call Thomas and tell him I have some more news to tell him. I'm sure he's getting tired of hearing me say those words, nothing good ever comes from it. I go straight to his house and I collapse into his arms. Thomas scoops me up and carries me to their couch.

"What's wrong?" Thomas asks me as his face fills with concern. "I found out more details about my stupid accident" I say. "Well what is it?" "Apparently, I was pregnant and I miscarried. I was so out of it, but Jake's mom pretended she was my mom to receive the news and then kept it from me this whole time." Thomas's mouth falls open, but no words come out. "I, wow. I don't even know what to say" he tells me. "How did you find out?" He asks. "My appointment. The doctor told me when she was recapping my medical history. She had no idea that I didn't know. When she mentioned it I had an anxiety attack." Thomas sits next to me and pulls me into a hug. "I'm so sorry Sarah. It's as if every time you start to get over that night, there's something else, even worse, that pops up." "Exactly!" I say a bit too excitedly and jump up. He gets it, finally someone understands. I can see Thomas eyeing me as I start to pace in front of him. "It's like I can't escape that night. Just when I think I'm getting over one thing, then bam, something else comes up" I say while clapping my hands together for emphasis. Thomas pats the cushion next to me, "Why don't you come sit down and try to relax? I know your mind has probably been going a hundred miles per hour today." I sit back down and make myself cozy next to him. "Have you told Jake?" He asks me. "No and I don't think I will" I tell him. "What? Why not?" Thomas asks a little surprised. "Because it's not going to make a difference either way. I am his past and Stacy is his future" I say bitterly as Ms. Henson's words roll off my tongue. "Yeah, but that's pretty significant. If it were me, I would still want to know. That way I could be there emotionally and mentally for the other person." Maybe Thomas has a point. "You really think so?" I ask. "I know so. With as much strife you've been put through, especially by his mother, Jake should know. You shouldn't have to carry this burden alone." I stare into Thomas' eyes and it's hard to imagine a time when Thomas treated the women he was with so poorly. The amount of love, compassion, and patience he has for me is unwavering and that's when the guilt hits me like a wave. How did I get so lucky to find another guy in this world that cares about me and treats me so kindly the way Thomas does? I lean into him and give him a kiss. "What was that for?" He says when I pull away. "Just being you" I say. "Well then I like being me" he teases.

I use this as an opportunity to change the subject. "Sooo, if you're not busy tomorrow, it would mean a lot if you helped me work their engagement party. As a volunteer" I quickly add. He gives me an exaggerated frown, "I can't babe. We have an away game tomorrow, otherwise I'd be there." Damn there goes that plan. Looks like I'm going to have to ride it out with Beth tomorrow. I feel my phone buzz and I pull it out prepared to see a distraught text from Jake about smacking his mom. It's Beth: *Sarah I really hate to ask this of you, but I was supposed to pick up some extra decorations for the party tomorrow. I'm not going to make it in till late, do you think you could get some for me? Please??* I let out a sigh which prompts Thomas to read the message over my shoulder. "Seriously?" He says aloud. "Just my luck" I say. "Yeah I don't think you should buy a lottery ticket any time soon" he says jokingly. I shoot him a glare, "I'm kidding. Here, come on" he says as he stands up and sticks his hand out for me to grab. I take his hand and he pulls me up. "What?" I ask. "Well I may not be able to help tomorrow, but I can go with you to do this" he tells me. I flash him a smile, relieved that I don't have to do this on my own.

By time we leave the party store, I've spent $50 and I'm really hoping Beth reimburses me. I did get a little carried away, but then I had to remind myself who it was for and dial it back. If this was for anyone else, I would have no problem letting my artistic abilities take over and offer to decorate the whole store. Being the snooty jerk Stacy is, she probably won't appreciate any of it or she'll tell Beth I did a horrible job just to spite me. We decide to stop by the store and drop everything off that way I don't have to carry it all in by myself tomorrow.

When we make it back to Thomas's I thank him and go to leave. Before I make it all the way to my car, Thomas calls out my name. I spin around and see him standing on his porch. Did I forget something? I start walking towards him and he meets me half-way. "What is it?" I ask. "Do you love me?" He asks. "That's a random question, but, um yes I love you." "Good. Just making sure" he says and follows it with a kiss. I give him a suspicious smile, "Okay…" I say slowly. He gives me a nervous chuckle, "I guess, I'll let you go now" he says. "Alright, I'll talk to you tomorrow" I tell him.

That was strange, I think to myself. Shopping for engagement stuff probably got him in a sentimental mood. I head home and escape to my room so I can properly decompress from today's revelation. I remind myself that I owe my mom an explanation, but I don't think I can handle talking to her right now. I really don't want to tell anyone else. I feel ashamed. I look in the mirror as I rub across my belly. I can't believe I was pregnant, how did I not even know? Would I have been a good mom? Probably not, Ms. Henson's verbal abuse did have some truth to it. I was off the deep end, partying almost every other night and succumbing to some bad habits. I have definitely been humbled over these past few months and it has allowed me to reevaluate my priorities in life. I realize now, I have been so selfish. I did treat Jake like my trophy. I flaunted him off to all my friends and used his popularity to make a name for myself. Don't get me wrong. I love Jake unconditionally, I would do anything for him. I just can't deny that loving him did have its advantages for me. Maybe Ms. Henson has been right all along, I'm not good enough for Jake. He deserves someone better, someone without selfish motives. I don't think Stacy is that person either and I'm not just saying that because of my distaste towards her. Just as I have myself convinced that Jake might actually be better off without me, Thomas's words pop up in my mind. Should I tell Jake, about our miscarriage? Would it really be beneficial for him to know. It could serve as a form of closure for me. That way I don't have to carry this burden with me the rest of my life, like Thomas said. Do I want to burden Jake with this kind of news though? It'll be easier if only one person has to live with it. However, I am just going to tell him and then move on. It's not like it's going to change anything either way.

Chapter 13

When I wake up, I reluctantly get out of bed and get dressed for school. I am not looking forward to this evening, but I wish it would hurry up so it could be over with already. I pack myself a bag for later with my uniform in it, because I won't have time to come back by the house after class. We will be closing the store to regular customers at five to set up for the party and then seven is when the party will begin. I hope Stacy leaves it to us to decorate because I don't want to spend anymore time with her then I have to. Not to mention, I need time to gather the courage to tell Jake about the miscarriage. I keep telling myself that once I tell him, we can both move on. Since I found out, it's all I can think about and Thomas is right, it'll help ease my mind some when I tell Jake. I've decided I need to somehow tell him after the party because I don't want him to be distracted during the party. Especially since the two people who despise me the most will gladly blame me for ruining the party.

Needless to say I am unable to focus in class, but I manage my way through. I really need to get all this behind me, because it's starting to take a toll on my grades. I have two months till the end of the semester and I need to get back on track so I can go into finals feeling confident. It's not like I'm close to failing, I just have never taken such pride in my classes and it hurts to see my grades slipping. I should've been this driven the first time around. Maybe I could've avoided this whole past year if I just walked the straight and narrow path to begin with. Of course it's easier to ask ourselves, what if? I should be asking myself what I can do to make the situation better or change the outcome.

I make it to the shop and get changed for work. There are four hours until we close to the public and I don't think I am ready for it. I try to clean up in-between customers so I can save some time later. I didn't realize until now that Stacy's parents will be here tonight and I can't help but wonder if Stacy has told them about me and Jake. Chances are she did and now I have two more people to add to my anti-fan club. I am curious how Stacy's father will behave tonight. He was pretty irate that night at the game. No wonder Stacy doesn't want to live with him, he seems like he has short temper. He should be pleased though, he got what he wanted, so did Stacy. I can definitely see who she gets her manipulation skills from though.

By time five rolls around, I finish up the last few customers I have and then lock up. It's time to start decorating and even though I hate to admit it, I actually enjoy it. I love decorating and planning parties. Part of me hopes that one day I can become an established party planner, once I get some business experience under my belt. That's why my goal is to be an executive assistant once I graduate. They are the planners and masterminds of setting up meetings, parties, and everything in between.

Beth shows up at six to help finish decorating and by time we are done, the shop looks posh yet homely at the same time. We did a good job of making it look festive and welcoming. As I'm admiring our handiwork, I notice that we only have less than an hour before the party starts. This means Stacy and Jake will be showing up any minute. I've already tried to mentally prepare myself for all the PDA Stacy will blatantly rub in my face throughout the night. It's an engagement party so naturally they should be acting all lovey-dovey. I wonder if they have made it to the 'I love you' stage yet.

A knock at the door brings me back to reality. "I got it" Beth says as she makes her way to the door to let Stacy and Jake in. I can feel myself get weak in the knees as Jake steps in. It should be illegal for a man to look as good as Jake. He has on black slacks and a black button down with a silver tie that I bought him for our second anniversary. I take a hard swallow and turn away once I catch myself staring. He probably doesn't even remember I gave him that tie. Stacy is wearing a silver cocktail dress that seems just a tad bit too tight on her and I'm sure it's because of the pregnancy. I wonder if everyone coming tonight knows that she's pregnant or if she is trying to play it off? That would explain why she came in a dress that doesn't fit her comfortably. Either way she looks uncomfortable and keeps tugging at the sides to pull it down. Her look of discomfort fades once she sees me and it's as if her eyes are set on a new target.

"Sarah, there's some more stuff in the trunk. Would you be a sweetie and fetch it for me?" She says with a devilish grin. I don't know what annoys me more. The fact she called me sweetie and she's younger than me or she used the word 'fetch' like I'm her little dog. "Sure" is all I say as I make my way outside. I open the trunk and see a box full of party favors and goody bags. I pick up the box and underneath are a few open condom wrappers. I grit my teeth and roll my eyes, I'm sure she planned that strategically. I carry the box back in and distribute the favors and bags amongst the table upon Stacy's request. Just as I finish up, the first guest arrives and from what I hear it's Stacy's Aunt.

Five minutes till seven everyone starts to show up. Amongst that crowd is Ms. Henson and she doesn't even try to hide the smug look on her face when she sees me. Hopefully I can avoid her for the duration of this party. Once everyone files into the shop I notice a woman and Stacy's father outside having what seems to be a heated argument. Afraid that he might treat the woman like he did Jake that night at the game, I step outside for back up. When they see me emerge from the shop they both direct their gaze towards me. "Can I help you?" Stacy's father says impatiently. "I'm sorry, but there is a private party being held here at the moment and we can't have anyone loitering outside the premises." The man lets out a huff showing his obvious annoyance, "I am aware. We are the parents of Stacy." That makes sense, but he doesn't need to be getting into an argument with her outside for others to hear. "Oh. Well I'm sure she's been waiting for you to arrive" I say motioning towards the door, hoping it would usher them in. "Thanks, we'll be in, in a minute" he says as he turns attention back to Stacy's mother. "Um, I'm sorry, but I can't really have anyone standing around out here. It gives the impression we are open for business." Of course I'm lying through my teeth, but I don't feel comfortable having people alone with this man. He shoots me a nasty glare and stomps his way towards the door. I wait for Stacy's mother to make her way in before I follow behind. "Are you okay?" I whisper to her. "Yes dear, thank you" she whispers back.

Once I re-enter the shop, I take notice how full and lively the shop is. There is music playing in the background and you can hear the low roar of multiple conversations taking place. It's not long before I spot the couple of the hour and I can't help but feel the sting in my throat as I see Jake with his arm around Stacy's waist and they are looking at each other laughing. "Don't they make such a cute couple?" I turn to see Mary standing behind me, it's evident she caught me staring. "I have work to do, excuse me." I say. "Oh, be a doll and refill my drink" she says as she shoves her empty cup in my hand. I hate that I don't even have to ask what she's drinking, because I already know. When I return with her drink she has Jake and Stacy in her company now. "Here's your drink" I say and turn to quickly to make my escape, but there's no such luck. "Sarah, would you mind taking our photo?" Ms. Henson asks. "Sure" I say through clenched teeth and a fake smile. I take her phone and wait for them to pose. Jake mouths 'I'm sorry' and gives me a half hearted smile. I wish he didn't have to be so considerate, it would make getting over him that much easier. I snap the picture and hand her phone back and then make a beeline into the crowd.

Right at eight Jake and Stacy make their way to the front of the crowd to make their toast. "We would like to thank everyone for coming out to celebrate mine and Jake's engagement. I am so glad everyone could show up to celebrate the love we share. I am so blessed to have such a handsome, caring man at my side that I will soon get to call mine for the rest of our lives." Stacy turns towards Jake indicating that it's his turn to speak. "Yes, thank you everyone for coming out. Your support means a lot and I can't wait to see everyone again on our wedding day when I get to marry this beautiful lady. If everyone could raise their glasses in the air and cheers with me. Here's to happiness and love" he says as his eyes land on me. "Kiss" the crowd begins to chant in unison. Jake and Stacy look at each other blushing and then give the crowd what they want. I turn my head and I can hear the crowd erupt with *oohs* and *awes* followed by the clinking of glasses as they finally finish their toast.

I make my way to the bathroom because I need a moment to myself. I am about to knock on the door when

I hear two voices bickering. I can hear Stacy's father and who I assume to be her mother. I put my ear up to the door to eavesdrop. "You should've never intervened" her mother hisses. "I'll be damned if that boy didn't own up to his actions. If he can knock her up, he can marry her damn it." "Forcing him to propose was wrong Jerry. Just because your parents did the same thing to us, doesn't mean you have to do it to your daughter" she replies. "It's the right thing to do Laura. They'll thank me later." "Oh really? How long do you think they'll last? Look at us, we ended up growing to resent each other and being unhappy." "This conversation is over" he says sternly. I quickly scurry away so I don't encounter the ever so pleasant Jerry.

I find Beth and help her take a head count of how many yogurts that have been served. "Hey you doing okay?" She asks. "Yeah, I'm hanging in there." Which is surprisingly true, I'm doing a lot better than I thought I would. "Good" she says, "would you mind cleaning that table over there. Looks like some kids spilt yogurt all over the table" she says giving a slight eye-roll. I let out a small chuckle, "yeah, no problem." I make my way over to the table and wipe it off. As I am walking back to the counter I hear a faint "Owe, let go." I look over and I see Stacy's father has his hand wrapped around Stacy's wrist. My instincts kick in and I quickly go over to them. "Let go of her" I say sternly. "Excuse me?" He says as he releases her from his grasp. "You shouldn't be putting your hands on a woman, especially one that is pregnant." "I don't know who you think you are to keep meddling in our business, but I suggest you back off if you know what's good for you" he says. "Maybe I wouldn't have to meddle, if you weren't picking on someone every time I see you" I reply. His face turns red and he opens his mouth to say something, but looks around knowing better than to cause a scene. He looks at Stacy, "I better not catch you taking another sip of champagne" he says and walks off. Stacy looks embarrassed. "Are you okay?" I ask. "I'm fine" she snaps. I decide to leave it at that, but as I walk off I hear her mutter "thank you."

Now I really need a break, I think to myself as I make my way back to the bathroom. Despite my obvious dislike towards Stacy, I couldn't just let her father treat her that way. No one deserves to be treated so harshly and that's why I went to her defense. As I am about to knock on the bathroom door, Jake emerges. "Hey" he says giving me his infectious smile. "Hi" I reply trying to cut the conversation to a minimum, but then all of a sudden it hits me. I need to tell Jake the news. "I have to tell you something, but it needs to be private" I tell him. He nods and then looks past me and I turn to see Mary has her eyes fixed on us. "That's going to be a bit difficult" he says cautiously. "I know, but it's really important" I say as the emotions start to flood through. Don't do it, I tell myself. Don't cry in front of all these people. "My mom is staying with me while she's in town, so, I will try to sneak away tonight. If not I'll swing by here tomorrow while you're working." "Okay" I say. "She's coming this way" he tells me. I nod and we part ways as I go into the bathroom.

This party is emotionally draining. Luckily there's less than an hour left because I don't think I can handle much more. I splash my face, hoping it'll make feel more refreshed. As I exit the bathroom Ms. Henson is standing there waiting. "All yours" I say, trying to play dumb. "Not so fast" she says. "What Mary? What now?" I say giving her a look of defeat. For a moment she is taken aback by my bluntness, but then she continues, "What were you and Jake talking about?" She asks. "First of all, none of your business. Secondly, no I haven't told him yet" I tell her. "If you were smart, you wouldn't tell him at all" she hisses, "look at them" she demands. I glance in there direction to see them, embraced in each others arms slow dancing. Their smiles seems bright and carefree. A wave of guilt hits me. Maybe telling him isn't such good idea after all. "What good would it really do? Except make it harder for Jake to move on?" Mary tells me. "It would help ease my conscious" I tell her bleakly. "Look Sarah, if I have to admit it. I am not exactly thrilled Jake is marrying Stacy either. I know we have always been at odds, but at least I knew his feelings for you were genuine. He hardly knows this girl, but now that she's pregnant he's trying to do the right thing and it's out of both of our hands." This was probably the most sincere

Ms. Henson has ever been with me. I just hate it had to come to something like this to force her hand. "Well, I guess you finally won" I say as I trudge off.

Great, now my doubts about telling Jake have returned. I guess Mary is right, it wouldn't make much of a difference besides making it more difficult on Jake. I need to suck it up and move on. Now I needed to think of something to tell Jake in place of my big secret. I start making my rounds to each table collecting all the cups, making a mental note of how many were used. As people start to leave I begin to wipe off the tables and chairs and start stacking the chairs so the others will get the hint. Eventually all that's left is me, Beth, Jake, Stacy, her parents, and Ms. Henson. Jerry, Stacy's father, is first to leave out of the mix. He makes his goodbye short and sweet and then leaves, but not before giving me a spine chilling glare. Once he leaves, I head to the back to gather the cleaning cart and make my way back out. When I return, Ms. Henson is gone and Stacy's mother appears to be saying her goodbye to Stacy and her now soon to be son in law.

I start taking down the decorations when I feel a tap on my shoulder. When I turn around I see Stacy's mother smiling at me. "Is it Sarah?" She asks. "Yes ma'am" I say sticking my handout for a shake. She ignores my hand and gives me a hug instead. "My name is Laura, I'm Stacy's mother." I already knew this though from eavesdropping on her and Jerry's conversation earlier.

"Nice to officially meet you" I tell her. She lets out a chuckle, "I just wanted to say thank for earlier. Stacy's father can be quite a hot head, but I appreciate you for looking out for me and I saw what you did for Stacy as well. I know there's some, uh, bad blood between you two, but that was very kind of you." So Stacy did tell her. "Not a problem" I reply, not knowing what else to say. It felt good though for someone to know our situation and not entirely hate my guts. Aside from Thomas that is, but then again his viewpoint is biased. "Anyways, thanks again" she says and then leaves.

Beth motions for me to come over and when I do so she gives me a soft smile. "I can stay and clean up if you want to head home? I know you've been here all day" she tells me. "Are you sure?" I ask hesitantly. "Absolutely. Go on, I got this" she says, giving me a reassuring smile. "Okay, well thanks" I tell her. I go and grab my bag and then leave without saying a word to Jake or Stacy.

As I'm getting in my car I feel a firm grip on my arm as it pulls me out of the car and throws me onto the ground. I look up and I see a mans figure standing over me. Before I manage to get up I receive a kick to the stomach which knocks the breath out of me, followed by a knee to the face. I fall onto my back, shocked and in pain. "Just take it" I say, while pitifully throwing my bag towards the man. I hear the figure scoff as if insulted him. My assailant kneels down next to me and I try to regain my vision in hopes of getting a good look, but he has a mask on. "Not so tough now are you? Next time you won't be so lucky." Holy shit, it's Jerry. That's my last thought before he punches me square in the face.

Chapter 14

When I come through, I'm laying in a hospital bed. I try to lean forward but a sharp pain radiates from my head all the way down to my back. "Owe" I cry out in pain. "Sarah" I hear Jake exclaim. I have a collar around my neck so I can't turn to see him. I see him dash to the door and he promptly returns with a nurse and doctor at his side. "Why hello Ms. Caldwell, I am your nurse, Britney, and this is Dr. Adams. We have been waiting for you to wake up so we could ask you some questions." "Okay" I try to say as my voice cracks from the dryness. "How long have I been out?" I ask. "It's hard to say for certain, because we aren't sure how long you were out before your friend found you, but it is 11:30pm as of right now" Britney replies. "Sarah, do you remember what happened to you?" Dr. Adams asks. My head feels fuzzy as I try to recollect my thoughts. My memory is hazy, but it all starts to trickle back in and a wave of uneasiness hits me as I begin to dry heave which only reminds me of the pain from being kicked in the stomach. "Go get her some Zofran" Dr. Adams tells Britney before continuing, "I need to have a look at you now that you're awake" he tells me. He makes his way over to my side and pulls out a penlight, "look right at my nose" he commands. He shines the bright light in my eyes, "great, now follow my finger using only your eyes." By time he finishes his exam, Britney returns with the medicine. "This should help you feel less nauseous" she tells me as she gives it through my IV. Wow, I can't believe I didn't wake up when they poked me. I must have been really out of it. "Can you tell me where you hurt?" The doctor asks. "Everywhere" I groan. "Can you try to be a little more specific?" He asks. "My head, my back, my stomach, and my knees" I tell him. "Very well. We already took some x-rays and a full body cat scan so we should be getting the results back soon. Would you like something for pain in the meantime?" "That would be nice" I say.

Once they both leave Jake rushes to my side. "Sarah" he says as tears start to well up in his eyes. "Jake, it's okay" I say as I rest my hand on his cheek. Even though it is a lie, I had to be strong. I couldn't let him now how much I hurt. "Who did this to you?" He asks angrily. I look away, unsure if I should tell him or anyone for that matter. Next time he will probably kill me. "Sarah, if you know who did this to you, you need to report it." I look back at him. "Where is Stacy?" "She's at home with her mom. We were walking out to the car when we found you" his voice fades as starts to choke up. "I was so scared, I thought I lost you. I hate seeing you like this." "What happened?" I ask, trying to play it off. "I don't know. You were just laying there, unresponsive. Your face was all bloody and your lip was busted and you have a swollen black eye. Stacy called 911 right away and it felt like an eternity before the ambulance arrived." "Who all knows?" I ask "Well, after Stacy called 911, she ran back to tell Beth and then I called your grandparents while we were waiting on the ambulance." Great I'm sure they are worried sick. "I think your grandparents are still in the waiting room if you'd like me to go get them?" He says as he rises up. "No, not yet. I don't think I can handle them smothering me right now." He nods and drops back down to my side. "So Stacy knows you are here?" "She knew better than to say anything. In fact, she told me to go with you when the ambulance showed up." I'm partly shocked, but part of me wonders if it's because Stacy has a hunch who did this to me and feels guilty. I'm not sure how to go about all this. If I press charges, then there's a chance I can get him locked up and he won't be able to hurt anyone again, but, what if he gets off and then comes for me with a vengeance? I shutter at the thought. "Are you cold?" Jake asks. "A little" I reply.

Jake gets up and leaves once more and returns with Britney, who has some blankets. "Here ya go" she says as she covers me up. "I have your pain medicine too." "Thank you" I tell her. "This is some pretty strong medicine and it might make you sleepy" she warns me. "That's fine, I could use some sleep" I say. "Before I give this to you, would you like to make a statement about what happened?" I become nervous and I look at Jake who gives me a nod of encouragement. "I'm scared" I say as I start to cry. Jake rushes to my side and grabs my hand, "I swear I will never let anyone hurt you again. Just tell us what happened Sarah." "Jerry" I say through my now uncontrollable sobs. The nurse looks at Jake, "Jerry? As in Stacy's dad Jerry?" Jack clarifies. "Yes" I say. "Would you like to press charges?" Britney asks. I try to nod which causes a sharp pain to shoot down my spine once more and they can tell by the grimace on my face. "Alright sweetie, just hang in there. I need to grab the doctor so you can give us the details and then I can give you the pain medicine." "Alright" I say as I sniffle back my tears.

Jake starts to pace the room. "I'm going to kill him." "Jake stop." "No! Who just beats another person senseless like that?" Jake says furiously. "The cops will handle it, Jake. Please don't do anything stupid. I don't need to be worrying about you when I'm stuck in here." He lets out a large huff, "Fine, but I'm not leaving you alone till I know he's taken into custody." "Good" I say. Jake's phone rings and he answers it quickly.

"Hey man, yeah I'm still here. She's awake now, do you want to talk to her?" Jake looks at me, "it's Thomas" he says. Great, I'm sure he is in a panicked frenzy. Jake puts the phone up to my ear and holds it there for me. "Hello" I say in a raspy voice. "Sarah, oh my God. Are you okay? We just made it back from the game. My phone had died, but I am on the way right now." "It's okay Thomas. I was unconscious so I wouldn't have known either way." "How are you feeling now? What have they said?" "I hurt all over, but I don't have any results yet. I'm still waiting to find out." "Alright, well I'll be there soon babe. I love you." "Alright see you soon" I reply. Jake hangs up the phone and puts it back in his pocket.

"That was nice of you" I tell Jake. "What?" Jake asks. "Letting Thomas know." "Ah, yeah, well, I hope he would do the same. I would want to be at your side as soon as possible." "I know" I say. His words fall a little heavier than they should, but I'm sure it's just because my emotions are heightened right now.

It's not much longer before Britney and Dr. Adams return and take my statement. I give them a synopsis of what happened during the party and then my account of what happened in the parking lot. By time I finish telling them, I am a blubbering crying mess and Britney fetches me some tissues. They inform me that when the cops arrive I will have to tell them the story once more, but now they can help fill in details in case I am too groggy from the pain medicine. Britney gives me the medicine and then leaves us alone once more.

We both sit there quietly until Jake breaks the silence, "What did you have to tell me earlier?" His question throws me off and quite frankly I had forgotten about the miscarriage for the first time since I had found out. Ms. Henson had convinced me not to tell Jake about it, but would this be a sign that I should? My hesitation reveals my internal struggle. "You know you can tell me anything, right Sarah?" "I know" I say reluctantly. "I just don't know how to tell you this and I hate that it has to be like this, so it makes me seem all the more pitiful." "Well if you want to wait then, I'll respect your wishes" he tells me. "Well, we may not get another opportunity alone like this" I tell him. "True" he says.

I let out a large sigh, "I went to the doctor yesterday and I found out some more news about our accident." "Okay..." he says slowly. "Turns out, I was pregnant at the time. I had no idea, but I guess I ended up miscarrying the baby." Jake's eyes fill with tears once again and he caresses my hand. "Why didn't you tell me as soon as you found out?" "I tried. I went straight to your apartment, but Stacy made it clear that y'all were, um, busy..." I tell him. I see his jaw tense up and I know he is mad, "She didn't even tell me you stopped by. That must have been when I went to pick up some groceries before my mom got there." "Well she made it seem like you two were in the middle of showering together." "Of course she did" he says in annoyed tone, before directing his attention back on me. "I am so sorry you had to go through this alone and to find out in such a shocking way." "I'd also appreciate it if you pretended like you don't know" I tell him. He gives me a puzzled expression, "What? Why?" "Because you're mother is the reason I never found out in the first place. She pretended to be my mom when the doctors came by to tell me the news and told them she would tell me when I woke up. Obviously she never did, That's why she freaked out and faked your death, she was scared about the close call and was desperate to keep us apart. She admitted it to me when I ran into her outside of you apartment that day and convinced me to not tell you." Jake is flushed with anger by time I finish explaining. "I wish I could say I am astonished, but at this point, that sounds exactly like something my mom would do." A silence falls upon us once more as Jake's face becomes riddled with sadness. "Sarah, I am so sorry. I feel like I have brought nothing but chaos, heartache, and pain into your life." "Jake, I wouldn't trade my love for you for anything." Our gazes lock and he gives me a weak smile as he brushes my bangs out of my eyes. I wince as he barely touches me and I can see the rage in his eyes. It's killing him not to go find Jerry and bring karma up to speed. "I love you and always will" he says. "I know, I love you too" I tell him.

A knock at the door startles us both. I feel myself holding my breath, until Thomas enters the room. The look on his face shows he is frantic and filled with worry. Jake rises up and kisses me on the top of my head. Jake turns and meets Thomas' gaze and they both give a nod of understanding. "Please keep an eye on her" Jake tells Thomas. I can tell he doesn't want to leave my side, but he's trying to do what's right. He turns to me once more, "Let me know what they say, okay?" He tells me. "Okay"

I reply. As he turns to go out the door he turns to face me once more and slyly holds up his hand and signs *I love you.* I had almost forgotten that was our thing. It's what he use to do anytime we were in class or from the field when I'd watch him from the bleachers. Was it instinct or has some of his memory come back? It was killing me to know.

"Babe, I'm so sorry it took so long" Thomas says, interrupting my thoughts. "It's alright, you're here now" I reply. He gives me a kiss on the forehead, replacing the one Jake gave me, and takes his place by my side. "How are you feeling? Have they given you anything for pain?" "Yes, they gave me some morphine. I think it's starting to kick in because, I don't feel as bad as a I did." "Good, I'm glad. Do you remember what happened? Jake mentioned that it looked like you got mugged." "Um...well, I didn't get mugged. He didn't take anything, except probably my pride, but I just got the crap beat out of me." I could see his hands clench to fists, "Who would do such a thing?' He says. "Jerry" I say flatly. "Jerry? Who the hell is that?" "Stacy's dad. I guess he didn't like that I kept him from putting his hands on Stacy and her mom." "That bastard. He deserves to rot in hell" Thomas says angrily. "I'll second that" I murmur. "So, what now?" Thomas asks? "Well, the police are supposed to be on their way to get my statement." "Good" Thomas says followed by a large huff and then says, "the nerve of that guy."

A soft knock directs our attention to the door and this time it's my grandparents. "Oh sweet pea" my grandpa exclaims, followed by a gasp from my grandma. They make their way over to me and my grandma takes my hand as she becomes tearful. "Sarah honey, how are you feeling?" She asks. "Much better now that I've had the pain medicine" I tell her."Is there anything we can do?" Grandpa asks. "Not really. We are just waiting. Waiting on the police and waiting on results" I say blankly. "Who on earth would do such a thing?" My grandma says in a bewildered tone. Part of me wishes I would have just addressed everyone at once because it is getting mentally exhausting telling everyone one by one.

By time I finish telling my grandparents the story, the police arrive to take my statement, so I start the process over once more. However, with the police I have to give gritty details and any extra information that I can remember. They even ask me questions I'm not able to answer. What was he wearing? What car did he drive? Is there any one who may have witnessed? I told them I wasn't sure because I was too busy getting the crap beat out of me. The older officer didn't seem to think that was very funny, but the younger one cracked a brief smile. I couldn't help but get snippy though. I hurt all over and I feel like all I've done is repeat myself for the past two hours.

"Thank you for your statement Sarah. We will get some officers over to his house immediately to bring him in for questioning. Is there anything else we can do for you in the meantime?" "Is there anyway to guarantee that he won't be able to come after me again?" I ask nervously. "You are welcome to file a restraining order in the meantime and if his bail ends up getting posted then we can notify you of his release." The thought of him getting let out and coming after me again makes me sick to my stomach. A puny piece of paper isn't going to stop him from coming after me, especially if I'm pressing charges on him. "If he is released, could one of you come stay with me? Like a stakeout or something?" I ask the officers with unease in my voice. "Ms. Caldwell I can assure you that the last thing a person with this accusation will do is try to come after you again. Most people look at it as getting off lucky and try to change their life around after this." Yeah, *most* people I think to myself. They don't know Jerry. They didn't see the look he gave me before he left the party and the hunger for violence in his voice before he beat my face to a pulp. "Okay" I reply, not really pleased with the situation at hand. "If they end up letting you go home tonight, you could try having someone stay with you, that way you'll feel more at ease" the younger officer states. What will make me feel at ease is knowing he is behind bars, I want to scream. "Thanks for the idea" I say before the officers leave.

Not long after the cops leave, the doctor comes in to reveal the damage. "Ms. Caldwell I think it would be best that we keep you here over night to monitor you. Your

CAT scan was reassuring. There is no brain bleed and no severe spinal injury. However, you do have a minor orbital fracture under your left eye that will luckily heal on its own. You also have whiplash and a concussion. I would not be surprised if you don't have what is called post-concussion syndrome for a week or so due to the direct trauma. So, you may feel dizzy, nauseous, and confused, along with having a headache on and off. I suggest you take it slow and easy. You are going to be hurting for a couple days, but I will prescribe you some pain and nausea medicine to go home with once you're released. Now do you have any questions for me?" Dr. Adams says. "I feel like I should, but I can't think of any right now." "Alright, well we will work on getting you to a room. In the meantime, I'll have Britney come in and take off the collar. Just be careful turning or moving your head because it will be very sore and tender."

Chapter 15

It's been two days since I was released from the hospital and I am still so sore. The pain medication helps just enough to take the edge off. To top it off, I just received a call that Jerry's bail was paid so now he's back on the streets and I'm sure he's angrier than ever. I try to hide the quivering in my voice when I call Thomas to tell him the news. As soon as I tell him, he informs me that he is packing a bag and coming over to stay with me until I feel comfortable. I don't even try to keep him from doing so, in fact I tell him to hurry. I'm not sure how long it will take me to get over this, but I need to figure it out soon because tomorrow is Monday and I have a presentation in my second class. I have basically put myself on house arrest and have not left the house since I got home from the hospital and now the thought of having to expose myself to the world tomorrow terrifies me. Granted, I emailed my professors about what happened and they have been understanding enough to give me extensions, but I'd rather not get behind, not this close to the end. A small part of me is also not looking forward to seeing Stacy either. I received a message from her while I was in the hospital that said *I'm sorry,* but that was it. I didn't reply because quite frankly, I don't know how to respond to her. Besides, the message was vague. Sorry for what? Sorry that your dad beat the crap out of me? Sorry that you've completely destroyed my second chance at happiness? I figure I'd save us both the embarrassment on Monday and skip my first class. Jake already told me he will come over to share his notes and let me know what I missed.

When I get off the phone with Thomas I immediately receive a call from Jake. "Hey where are you?" Jake asks frantically. "I'm at home in bed, why?" "Stacy just told me that her dad was released and I just wanted to make sure you were somewhere safe" Jake says. I take a hard gulp, "Yeah they just called to let me know" I tell him. "Do you feel comfortable or would you like me to come over?" He asks. "Actually, Thomas is already on his way over. I appreciate it though." "Oh" Jake replies and I can tell there is some disappointment in his tone. As difficult as it is, I can't let Jake lose sight of what's really important here. Stacy, which is now his fiancé, and their child. I know he wants to be here to comfort me, but if I let him then it'll just make the situation between us all the more confusing. I am vulnerable right now and I can't handle the pressure of trying to restrain myself around Jake. "I'll see you tomorrow though. Thanks again for taking notes for me." "It's not a problem. Please call me if there's anything else I can do for you" Jake says. "Will do" I tell him and then get off the phone.

When Thomas arrives I can't help but feel a sense of relief. Even I know it's silly to think that Jerry will break into the house to come after me again, but for some reason, I still feel paranoid. Despite being so sore, I make the journey downstairs to greet Thomas, but I don't think I can make it back up just this second. "Let's hang out down here" I suggest. While Thomas takes his bag up to my room, I make myself comfortable on the couch and turn on the TV. When he returns he plants a kiss to the top of my head and takes his spot next to me.

"How are you feeling today?" Thomas asks. "Still sore, but a little better than I was. "I just wish I could get rid of the headache and the aching along my side. It makes taking a deep breath hurt." Thomas gives me a frown, "I'm sorry babe." "It's not your fault" I reply. "I know, but if I could've been there like you wanted me to, then this probably wouldn't have happened." "Oh don't start this again. You had a game, it's not like you just blew me off. Besides if you wanna take the blame, get in line. Beth has not stopped checking on me. She feels horrible that she told me to go home when she did." "Gosh, I couldn't imagine being in her shoes" Thomas says. "I know. She keeps telling me she is so sorry and she is going to try to work something out with the owner so they give me paid time off." "Wow. That's really generous of her. Don't they only do that for full time employees?" Thomas states. "Exactly. I told her that it isn't necessary, but she insists." "Well then I guess there's no stopping her." "True" I tell him. "Have you eaten today?" He asks me. I give him a weak smile and replies with a scowl. "Sarah, you need to eat" he tells me and then stands up. "Where are you going?" I ask. "To make you something to eat" he replies. "You don't have to do that. I can have Esther make me something" I say, now feeling guilty that he feels the need to take care of me. "It's fine, really. It'll give us something to do." "Us?" I say rhetorically. He lets out a chuckle, "Yeah, I need to get you up and moving. I don't need you getting all stiff from lounging around" he says teasingly. "Hey now, that was doctors orders remember?" We both laugh.

After lunch we make our way up to my room so Thomas can work on his homework and I can finalize some details on my presentation. When Thomas finishes his homework he helps me put together my poster-board. Thomas may play it off like he's a hardcore masculine athlete, but he is actually very gentle and artistic once you get to know him. "Wow. This looks great" I exclaim once we finish putting together the board. "If you don't get an A, then they are crazy" Thomas tells me. "That's if I don't screw up my speech" I tell him. "You're going to do fine" he tells me reassuringly, before continuing, "do you want to do a run through now that you have everything together?" He asks. "Oh it's okay. I don't want to bore you with my lame research" I tell him. "Are you kidding? I don't mind at all. I'd love to hear it" he tells me. "Well, alright" I say, feeling prideful that he is interested in my work.

Once I finish my presentation Thomas gives me a round of applause. "Brilliant! You so got this" he tells me with a beaming smile. "Why thank you. I just hope it goes that smooth in class" I tell him. "Just pretend like I'm there, sitting in the back row, that way your gaze is directed on the class" "That's pretty clever" I say. "I know, I can be smart sometimes" he says with a chuckle. "How do you feel about getting back out into the world tomorrow?" He asks me. "A little nervous. I'm glad you're taking me though, otherwise I don't think I'd be able to muster the courage." "I won't let anything happen to you" he tells me and I reply with a kiss.

We spend the next couple of hours talking, laughing, and watching movies. It serves as a good distraction, but as we lay down to go to bed, all my uneasy feelings start to seep to the front of my mind once again. The longer I lay here, the more anxious I get. "Thomas?" I ask, hoping he's still awake, but to my luck, he's already asleep. I softly nudge him and he just rolls over and puts his arm around me. I lay there for another two hours, letting my thoughts consume me before my mind spares me and lets me fall asleep.

As the sun starts to creep through the curtains, I dread getting up. I look over and Thomas is still sound asleep. I force myself to get up and start getting ready since it's going to take me longer anyway. Appearance is ten percent of my grade, so I need to make sure I look good and professional. After I pick me out some slacks, a blouse, and a matching blazer. I make my way to the bathroom to fix my hair and put on some make up. The foundation I put on covers my black eye for the most part and I'm hoping my professor wouldn't deduct points for such a thing. When I finish getting ready I head back into my room and see Thomas is now up getting changed.

"Good morning" I say. "Good morning. Wow, you look stunning" Thomas replies. "Thanks babe." "Just give me a few minutes and I'll be ready" he tells me. "Sounds

good. I'm gonna go down and grab some breakfast then."
He gives me a peck on the lips and we part our ways.

I feel nauseous, but I force myself to scarf down
some eggs and toast. I try to focus on going over the key
notes for my speech, but right now my mind is elsewhere.
My mind keeps wandering to the thought of Jerry finding
me at school and finishing what he started. There's no
way he would be bold enough to do such a thing. Besides,
he doesn't know my classes and there will be plenty of
people around as witnesses. "Ready?" Thomas asks,
interrupting my thoughts. "Ready as I'll ever be" I tell
him. He puts his arm around and grabs my poster board
and backpack. "Well then let's go before you change your
mind" he says.

As we pull into the school parking lot, I perform my
deep breathing exercises to ease my nerves. I finally pull
myself together and get out of the car. Thomas walks me
to class and wishes me luck before he rushes off to class.
When I settle in my seat and look around at everyone else
rehearsing their lines, my nerves about Jerry fade away
and are quickly replaced with my fear of public speaking.
If I would've been in the right mind-set, I would've been
freaking out about this for the past three days, but I've
been a bit distracted.

When my professor walks in he is surprised to see me
and makes his way over to me. "Ms. Caldwell, I must say
I am surprised to see you. How are you feeling? Are you
sure you're up for this? I have no problem granting you

an extension." "Yes sir. I am feeling fine. I would prefer not to delay the inevitable. Besides I'd feel more comfortable presenting with everyone else instead of being the outcast." He lets out a soft chuckle, "Very well, I admire your dedication" he tells me and then heads up to the front of the room.

Once he gathers everyone's attention, we all draw a number so we know which order we will be presenting in. I draw number six and nervously await my turn. I always wonder, why do people get so nervous before presenting? If everyone is so nervous then chances are they aren't even focusing on you while you are presenting. They are more preoccupied going over their own presentation in their head and settling their own nerves. I mean, after all that's what I'm doing right now. I can't even focus on the speaker that's up there now. My heart is beating so damn fast and my palms are sweating like crazy, I couldn't even tell you what the main concept of her presentation is. When she concludes her presentation we all clap and then the next person goes up there. Now there's two more people before it's my turn.

Before I know it, it's my turn and I make my way up to the class and set up my poster board and pull up my powerpoint. Over the next fifteen minutes, I discuss the importance of data collection throughout the course of event planning and the positive correlation it has on customer satisfaction and how it results in increased business. I also explain that by using the data it can show the current growing trends for events and parties that people are interested in and things that people don't typically like. As I conclude my speech I feel like have been presenting for an hour, but I know that is a lie because the timer at the podium clocks me at fifteen minutes and thirty seconds. Perfect timing, every minute over we are penalized a point. Luckily no one has any questions, so I make my way back to my seat as they clap and the next person takes my place at the podium.

When everyone finishes presenting, the professor has us turn in our posters and then releases us early. I wasn't expecting to have free time and now that I'm on my own, my anxiety continues where it left off. I go straight to the cafeteria because it's a well populated area and I don't want to be alone right now. As I sit alone sipping my coffee, I start to regret not making any other friends. How would I have known things would have led to this though? I reflect on the simpler times before I found out Jason was Jake and Stacy didn't hate my guts. I only have myself to blame for pursuing Thomas so blindly. I can't say I regret it, Thomas has been beyond perfect, but it does seem a bit suspicious. Maybe I feel that way because of my own lack of honesty and dedication to Thomas.

Chapter 16

I get so lost in my thoughts that when I feel a hand on my shoulder, I nearly jump out of my seat and let out a shriek. I frantically rise from my chair to face the person and I am quickly relieved when I see that it's Jake. "I'm so sorry, I didn't mean to scare you" he says remorsefully. "It's okay, I'm just a little on edge. I thought you were…" my voice trails off, but he knows who I am talking about. "I know, I'm sorry" he tells me. We both stand awkwardly looking at one another until I sit back down. "Do you mind?" Jake asks motioning to the chair across from mine. "Not at all" I reply. "I didn't think I'd see you until later" he tells me. "Yeah we got out of class early. So, now I'm waiting on Thomas." "Ah, gotcha" Jake says somberly. "Do you have the notes from class? We can go over them now so it saves you a trip." "I wouldn't mind, but I don't think I could handle being in your room again." I immediately blush as I'm reminded of our last night together. "Good point" I tell him.

He pulls his notebook out and flips to the pages from today so I can copy them down. As I am copying the notes, I glance up and I see Jake staring at me. "What?" I ask. "Just admiring the view" he replies. "Oh" I say, not really sure how to reply to that. "Could you elaborate on what he meant by this part?" I ask in hopes of getting the attention off of me. Now I am the one distracted. As Jake explains the notes, I can't help but admire his jawline as he speaks and I become hypnotized by his eyes. It's as if he is speaking in slow motion, but I don't hear a single word he says. How could a human being be so handsome? "Does that make sense?" He asks, drawing me back to reality. "Um, yeah for the most part" I tell him.

When I finish copying the notes, we both sit silently as the room buzzes with life around us. Finally I break the silence as the curiosity consumes me, "So, where is Stacy?" I ask him. "She didn't feel comfortable coming today, since she knew it was your first day back" "Oh, well, that is considerate of her I guess." "Yeah, I suppose it is" he replies. "How are you two getting along?" I ask. "We're fine. How are you and Thomas?" "We are good" I tell him. "That's good." "Sure is" I say. "Go ahead and ask" Jake says, as if he knows what I'm thinking. "I don't know what you are talking about" I reply trying to sound dumbfounded, but simultaneously it crosses my mind if they have been intimate with each other. I swear if I was a cat, I would have been dead along time ago from all of my curiosity. "We haven't had sex" Jake says blatantly. "Well that's good" I say. "I mean not that you can't, she's your fiancé. I just meant that if that's what you want then that's cool" I tell him. I could see a smile tug at the corner of Jake's mouth as I finish my rambling. "Have you?" He asks me. The question throws me off because I don't want to lie to him, but I don't want to hurt him either. "Yes we have" I tell him. Jake takes a hard swallow and I can tell he's trying to keep his cool, but I can see the heart shattering look in his eyes before he looks away. Was I supposed to lie? He couldn't expect me to abstain from sex for the rest of my life, not after he slept with someone else. Hell, he even got her pregnant. "Oh, well good for you" he murmurs.

It kills me to know that since I told him, he won't keep holding out on being intimate with Stacy. Not after I've revealed that me and Thomas have taken our relationship to that level. After all, that's how we got in this mess the first place, Jake was upset because he thought I had slept with Thomas. Now that I have there's nothing holding Jake back. I mean I can't live in fantasy land. They are engaged, it's not like they are going to practice abstinence from here on out. I can't help myself, "You will always be the best though" I tell him. His eyes meet mine and for a brief moment it's as if I can feel the passion we share radiate between us, but then he clears his throat and quickly looks away. "Are you done?" He says as he picks up his notebook and puts it back in his bag. It makes me feel self conscious and I am about to ask him if he felt the same way, but I soon realize it wasn't what I said, it's because Thomas was approaching us.

"Hey you two" Thomas says. I turn around and give him a smile. "Hey" Jake says. "What are y'all up to?" Thomas asks. "Just got done copying the notes Jake took for me this morning" I reply. "Oh that's right, well how'd your presentation go?" Thomas asks. "I feel like it went okay. Our grades will be posted on Wednesday." "That's good" Thomas says. "Yeah that's good" Jake adds. "Well did you wanna stay and hang out for a bit or were you ready for me to take you back home?" Thomas asks. I look at Jake and he shrugs his shoulders. "I guess we can head back" I tell Thomas. "See ya around" I tell Jake. "See ya" Jake replies.

Thomas takes my hand as we walk to his car. "How do you feel?" He asks. "I feel alright. I think" I tell him. "Well I'm glad you were able to make it through" he tells me. "Me too" I say. "Did you want to stop and get anything to eat or what?" "Um, I'd prefer if we just went straight back." "You got it" he says. I feel guilty because I know Thomas loves to stop and get food on his way home, but I didn't want to take any chances of running into Jerry. For all I knew, he can be on house arrest until the court date, but I did not want to bet on it.

The court date is a week from today and I am not looking forward to being face to face with Jerry. However, I will be glad to move past this and get this all behind me. There are only three weeks that stand between me and getting away from here and starting over. I need to tell Jake, but I have been putting it off because quite frankly, I don't want him to know. I just want to disappear without a trace, that way he can move on fully. It hurts to even think about. He's been a big part of my life, the one thing that's been constant over all these years. The history and the passion we share has always convinced me that we are supposed to end up together and that's why I have to go. We'll never be able to fully let each other go, so it's up to me to put an end to this.

"Earth to Sarahhhh" Thomas sings. "Huh? What?" I say as I come back to reality. "We are here. Are you feeling okay?" He asks me with concern in his tone. When I look around, I notice we are in my grandparents driveway. I can't believe I zoned out so hard. "Yeah sorry. I didn't sleep good last night with my nerves and all, so I think I am just exhausted, especially with it being my first day back out in civilization." "Okay. You scared me. I called your name like three times and you didn't even blink." "I'm sorry babe" I say giving him a soft smile. "Well, let's get you inside so you can take a nap" he says. "That sounds like a great idea" I tell him.

When we make it in the house my grandma rushes up to us. "Sarah come quickly. You received some flowers today and I must say it seems a bit strange." "What do you mean grandma?" "Just follow me and you'll see." We follow my grandma to the kitchen and she shows us the bouquet of flowers resting on the counter. "Thomas you are so sly" I say giving him a smile. "Babe those aren't from me" he says and my smile quickly fades. I grab the card and read it aloud. *"Glad to see you back on your feet. Sincerely, your secret admirer."* I look up mortified. "What the hell" Thomas says, "who sent these?" My breathing turns shallow and I grab ahold of my chest as it starts to tighten. "My valium" I say breathlessly. Thomas runs to my purse and comes back with my bottle of

Valium as my grandma gets me a cup of water. "In through your nose, out through your mouth" Thomas says as he softly grazes his hand up and down my back. "They must be from Jerry" I finally manage to say. "Oh my, that's what I was afraid of" my grandma says. "Then we need to report this" Thomas says. "There's no proof, they will probably just scoff at the thought, especially since it's not a threat." Thomas lets out a frustrated sigh. "Well then what do we do?" He asks. I snatch up the flowers and walk over to the trash can and throw them in and I rip up the card and throw it away too. "That's what" I say. I'm trying not to show it, but on the inside I am still panicking. Those flowers were obviously hand delivered, which means he knows where I live. I did not want to say it flat out and cause any more worrying, but I am going to have to play it extra safe. Just three weeks I tell myself. "I think I'm ready for that nap now" I tell Thomas. He nods and gives me a kiss on the forehead. "I'll walk you up to your room, but while you nap I am gonna have to go home and check in and grab a change of clothes." "Alright" I tell him.

I have to pretend that I am asleep before Thomas will leave my side. When he leaves I roll onto my back and stare at the ceiling. I should have known that I wouldn't be able to sleep after an incident like that. All I can think about is that Jerry knows where I live and I'm sure his little stunt is his way of letting me know that he can get to me if he wants to. Maybe it isn't safe for me to stay here after all. I wonder if I can go stay with Thomas. I pull out my phone to text him, but I'm supposed to be asleep so I decide to wait till he gets back to ask him. Instead, I find myself texting Jake.

Pretty sure I got some flowers from Jerry today. Not even a minute after I send the text, I receive a call from Jake. "Hello" I say. "What do you mean?" Jake asks. "When I got home, my grandma said someone dropped off some flowers. They weren't sent officially, it was a bouquet that you'd buy from the store and the card said, Glad to see you back on your feet. Sincerely, your secret admirer." It gives me chills just repeating it. "That bastard, how dare he" Jake says. "I know. It sent me into a panic attack." "I'm sorry. I wish I could be there to comfort you. I take it Thomas isn't there." "No he left to get a change of clothes after I settled down." "Ah, I see. Well, how are you holding up? I'm sure you're freaking out now that he has shown he knows where you live." Yes, I knew he would understand. Jake always knows what how I feel and what I'm thinking. "I am pretty spooked, I'm not gonna lie. In fact, I was hoping Thomas' parent's would let me stay over there for a couple days." "Um, yeah. That probably wouldn't be so bad of an idea" Jake says but I can hear the reluctance in his voice. "I just feel like this is Jerry's way of saying check mate, ya know?" "Yeah I understand. Just know my door is always open too, if need be." "Thanks Jake, I appreciate you" I tell him. "Of course. I would do anything for you" he tells me. "I know" I say as I feel myself smiling like a fool. You idiot, you can't keep doing this, I think. "Well I'm going to try and take a nap now. Thanks for talking to me" I tell him. "Alrighty and it's my pleasure" Jake says.

Chapter 17

I was discouraged to find out that I couldn't stay with Thomas because he found out his grandparents were coming down to visit. Which also meant he couldn't stay with me and needed to be back home by Wednesday. His parents said I could come over as much as I wanted, I just couldn't stay the night. I guess his grandparents are extremely old fashioned and would have a stroke if I were to spend the night. It amazes me how progressive Thomas's parents are with how strict his grandparents are. I just don't get why they have to pretend like they abide by the same rules. I guess I'll just cherish tonight and tomorrow with Thomas.

The next morning I am slow to get up. I feel so sluggish from the lack of sleep over the last few days and I don't want to get out of bed. Thomas rolls over and smothers me with kisses and I can't help but giggle at his method of trying to get me up. "I don't wanna get up" I sigh. "I know, but the sooner we get up and go to class the sooner we get to come back and snuggle" he says as he caresses my back and gives me a kiss. "That sure is tempting, but why wait when we could just skip straight to the snuggle part now" I reply. "As much as I would like that, I have a game today so I can't miss class." "Ugh, fine" I say teasingly as I get out of bed.

When we make it to school I decide to go spend my time in the courtyard and do some studying till my class starts. I should've known that wouldn't last long, because thirty minutes into my studying Jake finds me. "Can I sit with you?" He asks tensely. "Um sure" I say motioning for him to sit. "How's it going?" He asks. "It's going. Is everything okay? You seem off" I reply. "Uh, not really" he says nervously. "What's wrong?" I ask. "Well...Stacy finally chose the wedding date." "Okay, and?" I say. "She chose January fourth..." Jake says bleakly. I instantly become distraught. "Excuse me?" I reply. "I didn't even tell her that was our day or anything. I figured that would only make her stick with it even more. I asked her if we could maybe do it the following week or the week before or even the day before, but she said no. She doesn't want to wait much longer or she won't fit into any cute dresses and the week before is her parents old anniversary and she doesn't want it done then." "I hate her" I say, "I hate her so much. She is literally living the life I could've had." "And it's all my fault" Jake says depressingly. I want to comfort him and tell him, no it's not true, but it find of is. He's the one who got Stacy pregnant and has to own up to the actions. The only thing that could've prevented this, is if I would've left Thomas as soon as me and Jake knew our feelings for each other. "Well, it is what it is" I say, trying to neutralize the atmosphere. That was supposed to be *our* day, now I will never be able to look at that day the same.

"I'm really sorry Sarah." "No need to be sorry, Jake. You tried to fix it, but Stacy is stubborn. We both know that." "True" he says. "How are you feeling today?" Jake asks as an attempt to change the subject. "Hardly slept, but I'm hanging in there." He frowns, "I wish there was something I could do to help." "Just being a listening ear, is plenty" I tell him. "Well, that sounds reasonable. So how long are you going to be staying with Thomas?" He asks. "Actually, I won't be staying with Thomas. His grandparents are coming in this week so I am going to tough it out on my own" I reply. "I don't like the idea of you being alone, not after a stunt like that." "I know, trust me. I don't feel comfortable with it either, but I think I'll be okay for a couple days." "Okay, but if you need me to, I can come stay with you. Strictly platonic, I'll even sleep on the floor" he says. I take a long pause to make it seem like I'm considering his suggestion even though I already know my answer is a big fat no. Not because I don't want him to. I would love for nothing more, but I know that being alone with him is a dangerous game to play. "I think I'm going to try and tough it out, but if I change my mind I'll call you." "Sounds good" he says. "Anyways, I need to head to class" I tell him. "Alright, later."

By time Wednesday rolls around I am feeling a little more anxious about Thomas not being around. He has practically been at my side since I've been home from the hospital. Part of me is glad, because I think he needs a good breather from me, but the selfish part of me is worried about myself. "Good morning" he says. "Good morning" I reply and I can tell he is shocked that I am actually awake before him. "I bet you didn't even sleep" he says. "Of course I did. A whole four hours" I reply. He rolls his eyes, "What am I going to do with you?" "Hmm, maybe next time you can help put me to sleep" I say seductively. He groans, "Of course you'd say that the day I have to go back home." I give him a wink, "the anticipation is the best part." He replies with a kiss and we both get up and get ready for the day.

Thomas offers to drive me to school one more time and suggests that on the way home we stop by his place so I can meet his grandparents. I politely deny and tell him I don't think I'm in the right mindset to meet his grandparents. Besides as much as I've enjoyed having him over, I haven't been able to concentrate on studying. I need some good quality studying time so I can go into finals feeling confident. We drive separately to school, but Thomas still walks me to class and he gives me a longer than usual kiss when we part ways. I think he's pretty bummed about having to be away from me too.

As it gets closer to time for class to start, Jake shows up with Stacy at his side, of course. Jake gives her a parting kiss and I make eye contact with Stacy when they pull away. I'm glad I didn't bother putting on make up today so she can see the beautiful black eye her father had gifted me. She quickly looks away and scurries off. Good, I hope she feels like scum. I know I have been hard on Jake, but Stacy isn't exactly innocent either. It takes two to tango and she has definitely made this the longest and most complicated routine of tango I have ever seen.

Jake takes his seat next to me and when I face him I can see the look of sadness and anger flicker in his eyes. "How is your pain?" He asks as he grazes my cheekbone with his thumb. "It's more tolerable. I'm down to two pain pills a day." "That's good." I don't know what to say because, his touch instills a slight bit of pain, but at the same time his touch makes me numb. I find myself staring at his lips, wanting to kiss them and it's as if he's thinking the same thing because he trails his thumb down and traces it over my lips. I could feel myself starting to lean in towards him, but I quickly pull away and clear my throat. "So, um did you finish your paper yet?" I ask. "Not quite. I have my conclusion and references to do and then I'll be done." "Good, good" I say and then we both fall silent. That was a close one, I don't know what has overcome me. Luckily the professor enters the room and greets the class at this time.

When class is over we leave without saying another word to each other. It's saddening how nothing is the same anymore. Usually we would go have lunch together, but now that's Stacy and his thing. I shouldn't let it bother me, after all, it gives me some alone time to study. It's just unsettling how temporary things are in life. However, I guess that's what is so reassuring about life too because that means the bad times are only temporary too. I guess life is all about continuously searching for that perfect balance of content.

After my last class, I head straight home. When I make it home, my grandparents are waiting for me in the living room. "Sarah, we are glad you're home. We need to talk to you" says my grandfather. "Okay…" I say suspiciously. "Your grandma has another business trip that she has to leave for tonight. With everything that has happened, we know you probably don't feel comfortable staying home alone. It's no worry though, we can make arrangements for you to come with us." "Can it wait till tomorrow evening? I have a test tomorrow that I can't miss" I tell them. "Unfortunately not sweet pea. There has been an urgent last minute change so we would have to leave tonight in order to make it in time." I start to feel hot and queasy. Of course this would happen on the night that Thomas had to go back home. "Well I can't go with you then" I tell them reluctantly. They exchange a concerned look. "Ralph, how about you stay here with Sarah? I will be okay on my own" my grandma says to my grandpa. He replies with a nod. Great, now I feel like a jerk. "It'll be fine" I say with the most convincing tone I can muster, "Jake is coming over anyway to go over some homework so I'll see if he can just stay over." I say aloud and then realizing what I have said. Looks like my mind has decided for me. My grandparents look at each other once more and I can tell they are trying to hide their look of bewilderment. "Are you sure sweetie? I don't mind if your grandpa stays." "No it's fine, really" I say while giving them a reassuring smile. "Well… alright, if you say so" says my grandpa. "Hector will be here too, if that makes you feel a little better." "Yes, that makes me feel even better" I tell them. "Good, well we are going to start packing. Let us know if you need anything" my grandma says. "Will do" I say as I give them each a hug and they go about their business.

"What did I get myself into?" I mutter under my breath. I head up to my room and plop down onto my bed. It's not like I can tell Thomas my plan, he would freak out. Rightfully so too. I couldn't say I would be okay with one of his exes spending the night with him. I guess I need to ask Jake if he's up for it in the first place. I start to text him, but decide I should call instead.

Jake answers on the second ring, "Hello." "Hi, do you have time to talk?" I ask. "For you, always." Oh my, this may not be a good idea after all. "So, my grandparents are going out of town tonight and I was wondering if I could take you up on that offer after all."

"Absolutely. What time would you like me to come over?" "Anytime after six will be good." "You got it, see you then." "Great, thanks" I say. I can't believe I'm actually doing this. I should have just toughed it out. After all it's not like I'd be completely alone, Hector will be here, but what's done is done.

My grandparents are getting ready to leave when Jake is dropped off. "Bless his heart, when is he going to get a car?" My grandma whispers to me. "I'm not sure" I say as I wave to greet him. He gives me a small wave and flashes me his knee weakening smile. "Hi there Mr. and Mrs. Caldwell" Jake says as he greets each of them with a hug. "Well hey there Jake, long time no see" my grandpa says. "Where are you two off to this time?" Jake asks. "New York" my grandma says excitedly. "Yes, now you know why I have to go with her. Otherwise she'll try to come home with a chunk of the big apple herself" my grandpa adds. We all laugh. "Safe travels" I tell them as I give them each a kiss on the cheek. "Of course. You two behave" my grandpa says and then gives a nervous chuckle at the realization of what he just said.

After we see them off, me and Jake head inside. "Have you had dinner yet?" I ask. "No. Have you?" "No, but Esther is making dinner now" I tell him. "Wonderful, I came at a good time then" he says as he pats his belly, which makes me laugh. "Where should I put my bag?" He asks. "Whichever room you'd like" I tell him. "So, your room?" He says giving me a mischievous grin. I give him a stern look, "I'm kidding. I'll take the room next yours" he replies. "Alrighty. I'm gonna go watch some TV while you get settled" I tell him.

It's not long before he comes back down and takes his place at the opposite end of the couch. We both sit there for about thirty minutes without making a sound, until Esther comes and tells us dinner is ready. Over dinner we make conversations about how our classes are going and how eager we are to graduate. This would be a good time to bring up my intentions of moving away, but I can't bring myself to do it. It'll be easier if I just leave without saying a word so he doesn't try to convince me otherwise. He tells me about how he plans on going back to school to pursue a degree in marine biology and it pulls on my heart strings to know that the Jake I know is still in there. It makes me wonder if he's still seeing a psychiatrist to regain his memory, but surely he would've told me.

When we finish dinner, I end up taking one of my pain pills to help the aching all over. I think my body isn't taking to kindly to me exerting myself. It's crazy how getting the crap beat out of you puts such a toll on your body. I intended to go upstairs and study for my test tomorrow but I don't think I can make it up the stairs. "Would you mind bringing me my backpack?" I ask Jake. "Sure, no problem" he says and then disappears to retrieve my backpack. I know I have about a good hour before my pain pill takes effect and knocks me out. When he returns, he hands me my backpack and then pulls out one of his books to read and makes himself comfortable on the couch. I utilize the time to review some of the processes that I don't feel too sure about and go over some practice formulas. As it approaches eight-thirty I can feel myself getting drowsy so I decide to call it a night. I put my stuff away and stand up to go to my room, but I fall back down into my seat. Well I can tell the pain med has kicked in because it always makes me a little woozy.

"Are you okay?" Jake asks as he comes over to me. "Yeah I think I just stood up too fast" I tell him as I stand up again and steady myself, "I think it's time for me to go to bed though." In one swift motion Jake sweeps me off of my feet. "What are you doing?" I ask. "I'm taking you to your room. I'm not gonna risk you falling down the stairs." I know better than to argue so I wrap my arms around his neck and let him carry me. When we make it to my room he lays me on the bed and as I slide out of his arms, it takes everything in me to let go of him. "Goodnight" he says to me and then kisses my forehead. I want to tell him to stay, stay and lay with me and hold me tight, but I watch him walk out.

When he leaves I manage to change into some pajamas and lay back down. The pain pill helps me fall asleep fast, but I am quickly awakened by a loud sound. It takes me a minute to realize it's the doorbell. I look over at the clock and it's 12:15 am, who in the world could that be? A sudden knock at my door startles me further. "Sarah are you in there?" Jake asks. I let out a sigh when I realize it's just Jake. I get up and open my door, to see Jake standing shirtless in front of me. "What's going on?" I ask. "I don't know, I think someone rang the doorbell. Stay here and I'll go check and see." "Are you crazy? I'm not staying up here by myself" I tell him frantically. "Fine. Follow behind me then." We make our way down the stairs and when we make it to the entryway, we see Hector standing there with a horrified look on his face and a bouquet of flowers. "What is it Hector?" I ask. "Miss Sarah, we must call the police" he says as he holds up the bouquet to reveal a bundle of dead flowers and hands me the card.

Roses are red, violets are blue, these flowers are dead-just like you.

Sincerely, your secret admirer

I feel sick to stomach and have to sit down on the chaise lounge. "That sick bastard" Jake says angrily. "Hector will you go get the phone?" Jake asks. Hector nods and hurries off. "Just breathe" Jake tells me as he cups my hands in his. Hector quickly returns and hands Jake the phone. I am so shocked I don't even know what to say, but luckily Jake takes charge. "Yes sir, I would like to file a threat that was just made" Jake says. Jake spends the next couple of minutes explaining what happened and they inform him they'll send a unit out to come check everything out. "They'll be here in twenty minutes" Jake says when he hangs up the phone. I go up to him and give him a hug. I start to cry and he squeezes me a little tighter. "Hey, look at me" Jake commands. I sniffle back some tears as I meet his gaze. "I swear to you, I will never let him hurt you again." I give him a pitiful nod and he pulls my head to his chest and it almost instantly soothes me. I can hear the faint sound of his heart beat and feel the warmth of his skin radiating to mine.

When the cops arrive we give them an account of what happened and they take the flowers and card as evidence. That ask me if I have anyone in mind who would make such a threat and I inform them of my open case against Jerry. They tell us that they'll keep a stake out for a couple hours to see if anyone tries to come back and to let them know if we notice anything suspicious going on in the house. The way they phrase it makes me paranoid. Could Jerry have gotten into to the house somehow without us noticing? We let the officers out and then we make sure to lock the door and check all the doors and windows.

Once we've thoroughly checked the first floor, Hector retreats to his room and leaves me and Jake alone. "I can stay up and keep any eye out so you can get some sleep?" Jake suggests. "I don't know" I say uncertain. "Come on" he says as he picks me up and carries me to my room once more. "If I notice anything fishy, I'll wake you up." He tells me. As he goes to leave, I panic "Wait." He looks at me but doesn't say anything. "Could you…" I start say, but trail off. I don't need me to finish my question, he knows exactly what I am asking. He walks over to the bed and lays down. The minute he gets in the bed I can feel his warmth again and I hate to admit it, but I find myself cozying up next to him.

I'm not sure who this is more torturing for, him or me, but I don't care. It feels so nice to have him close to me again. Even if it is temporary. His aroma lingers in the air and it is almost seducing in itself. How could someone smell so good at one in the morning? I roll onto my side to face away from him in hopes of subduing my hormones that are starting to rage. How am I ever going to get to sleep? "Goodnight" he whispers. "Goodnight" I tell him. Jake rolls over and puts his arm around me. I lay there, not wanting to move a muscle, in fear that it'll cause him to pull away. I also don't want to make any sudden movements so he doesn't think I'm trying to pull a move. I lay there for about fifteen minutes before I fall back asleep and that's how I stay until the morning.

Chapter 18

I must have been sleeping hard because I don't wake up until my alarm clock goes off. When I open my eyes I find myself lying on Jake's chest with my leg wrapped around him. I quickly sit up, embarrassed that my body would betray me. "Good morning" Jake says in a low raspy voice. "Good morning" I reply. "I'm so glad you're up because I don't think I could've held my pee much longer" he tells me. I give him a confused look, "why didn't you just go to the bathroom?" "You looked so cute, I didn't want to wake you" Jake says, which makes me smile.

As he leaves the room, I get up and start getting dressed. I can feel myself smiling like a lovestruck buffoon until I remember the horrendous ordeal that took place last night. I wonder how long the cops stayed and if they ever found Jerry and brought him in for questioning? He is one twisted creep. I can't believe that guy is going to be the grandfather of Jake's child. The thought makes me shutter. "Are you cold?" Jake asks. I turn to see him standing in the doorway and I instantly fall victim to his presence. The sun is peaking through the blinds and casts a ray upon him that emphasizes his tan muscular physique which is complimented by his messy, but cute, bed head. "No, but are you? Why don't you put on a shirt or something." I say a little more hostile than I mean to. "As you wish" he says with a delayed smile. Great, now he knows he got a rise out of me.

When we both finish getting ready, we meet downstairs for some breakfast. "You look nice" Jake tells me. "Thank you. I guess I do look pretty good for a walking corpse" I say lightheartedly. He gives me a stern look, "Don't joke like that." "Sorry. I'm just trying to lighten the mood" I say. "I don't see how because the world would be a much darker place without you in it" he says while taking a step closer to me. The decreased distance between us makes me slightly uneasy, but only because I don't know if I'll be able to control myself much longer. "Well now you know how I felt" I tell him. "Ya know, we could always fake your death too, so we can both just runaway together." Now I give him a stern look, "You know I can't do that" I say. "I know, but wouldn't it be nice?" He says whimsically. "Yes, yes it would be" I tell him. Jake is now within arms reach of me and I'd be lying if I said I didn't want him to come closer. I start to imagine how it would feel to kiss him just once more when the sound of my phone ringing makes me jump. I pull my phone from my pocket and see that it's Thomas.

"Hey Thomas" I say as I place my finger to mouth indicating for Jake to be quiet. "No that's alright. Jake was needing a ride today anyway so I told him I'd pick him up. Thanks for the offer though. Alright see you later." I hang up the phone and Jake gives me a smirk. "What?" I ask. "So are we back to sneaking around now?" He asks optimistically. "No...I just thought it would be best not to tell him that my ex-fiancé is staying the night with me." "But it's for your best interest and quite frankly, it's a good thing I was here given the circumstances of last night." "I know, I know. Now I am going to have to tell him anyway thanks to last nights fiasco. I am so glad you were here though, I don't know what I would've done without you" I tell him. He gives me a half smile, "Your grandparents should really look into getting some surveillance cameras. I'm honestly shocked they don't already have some" he tells me. "I know, that would be smart. To be honest I don't even feel comfortable staying here. At least not until the court date and I find out what the verdict is." "So what are you going to do?" He asks me. "I'm not sure. I don't really have anywhere else to go and I can't stay with Thomas until his grandparents leave." Jake gives me an upset look. "What?" I ask. "You could stay with me until you're able to go to Thomas's?" He suggests. I let out a small chuckle, "You can't be serious?" I tell him, but his face is stern. "Do you really think that's a good idea?" I ask him. "Well, of course I'm going to think it's a good idea. I know it puts us in an awkward situation, but, I'm not doing it because I'm trying to trick you into getting back with me. I'm doing it for your safety because I care about you and I don't want to see you get hurt, or even worse, killed." His last words are ominous and is what ultimately convinces me to agree. "Alright, I'll do it" I tell him hastily.

I can't believe I agreed to go stay with Jake. How am I going to break this to Thomas? I head up to my room to pack a bag before we head to school. My heart is already fluttering at the thought of being alone with Jake. Control yourself, I think. By Sunday I'll be able to go over to Thomas's, I just have to make it through the next three days. I decide that I should wait till I get to school to tell

Thomas, it's better to do it in person. Maybe I can play it off that I just found the flowers this morning? That way I don't have to tell him about Jake being over last night. I am such a big fat liar, poor Thomas. I wish I could be the perfect girlfriend for him, but all my conflicting emotions keep getting in the way.

By time we make it to school, I don't have time to meet up with Thomas beforehand so we agree to meet for lunch. I notice as Jake parts his way to go to class he appears to be a little chipper this morning and I'm sure it's because he is finally getting his way. As I'm walking to class I get a call from the police department informing that they have Jerry in custody and he's being questioned as we speak. I guess they found him at a bar near the house. They couldn't disclose the exact location, but did tell me that it is within proximity of my grandparents neighborhood.

When I finally make it to class, there are so many things on my mind that it makes it hard to focus. I try my best to take notes, but by time class is over I only have a page and a half of notes. Looks like I'll need to do some thorough reading over todays content to catch up on what I missed. I head to the courtyard to meet Thomas and mentally prepare myself to tell him my plan. I hope he doesn't croak when I tell him.

"Hey beautiful" Thomas says as he approaches me. "Hey" I reply. "How are you?" He asks. I give him flat smile, "Not too good. We need to talk" I tell him. Thomas quickly takes a seat next to me, "Okay, what's up?" He asks nervously. "This morning I went to leave the house and I found another bouquet of flowers, except these were dead and the card read roses are red, violets are blue, these flowers are dead, just like you and it was signed by my secret admirer again." "Babe, oh my gosh! I am so sorry. What did you do? Did you call the police?" "Yes I did. They called me when I got too school and told me they picked Jerry up at a bar near the neighborhood, so he's in custody right now." "That sick freak" Thomas says angrily. "I know, it gives me goosebumps just talking about it." "Well I am so sorry you had to go through that by yourself" Thomas tells me. "Yeah, it was, um rough. Which by the way, I need to talk to you about that." "About what?" He asks. "Being by myself. I know you are stuck at your house right now, but I don't feel comfortable staying at my grandparents given the situation. Do you think it would be okay if I stayed at Jake's the next three nights? I wouldn't ask such a thing if I didn't really feel as uncomfortable as I do." Thomas is silent and turns his gaze towards the ground. I can see he is struggling with the thought, and I'm sure he wants to tell me absolutely not. After a minute of internal debate, Thomas looks at me and lets out a large sigh. "I can't say that I am thrilled with the idea, but at the same time I don't want to be that asshole that tells you can't do something just because of my own insecurities. Especially, if it is something that is going to make you feel better and more at ease. With that being said, you do what you need to, but please don't invalidate what we share, that's all I ask." I cup his cheek in my hand and give him a soft smile, "I wouldn't jeopardize our relationship. After all, look how loving and kind you are to me. Plus, Jake is engaged." He smiles back at me, "I just can't help but get a little jealous when I think about you two together. You two share so much history together and I can't help but feel like some new chump that came along and got in the way." "Are you kidding me? Me and Jake have both made the decisions that have gotten us to where we are right now. We may share history, but there's a reason it's history. It's in the past. Life brought me to you and I didn't have to pursue my feelings for you, but I did. I won't lie, I can't say that I'll stop caring about Jake, but that doesn't mean I can't care for you too." Thomas takes my hand and holds it, "I love you Sarah and I have never felt the way I do about you with someone else, that's why I am scared of losing you." I reply with a kiss, "Trust me, I know how you feel and that's why it has been so difficult for me. Love isn't something you can just switch on and off" I tell him. "I know" he says glumly. "But hey, Sunday we will be together again" I tell him cheerfully and he gives me another smile. "It seems like an eternity away though" he tells me.

It feels so good to know that Thomas is okay with me staying with Jake. Well, I know he's not okay with it, but it's just relief to now that I don't have to lie about where

I'm at or hide what I'm doing. Now, Stacy on the other hand, she can't know what is happening and I made it clear to Thomas too. If she knew that I was staying over at Jake's she would probably have no problem letting her dad kill me, if she didn't beat him to it, that is.

Once Jake gets out of his last class we head to his apartment and I must say it feels a little strange being here. It's weird to think back to when we were still in Kentucky and had planned on me moving in with him so we could restart our life together. It's surreal how quickly things change. "You can stay in my room and I'll sleep on the couch" Jake tells me. "Are you sure? I don't mind sleeping on the couch." "Seriously? You think I'm going to let you sleep on the couch?" "No, I just already feel bad for intruding" I tell him. "Well don't. I'm glad I can help. Besides we haven't really got to spend much time together lately so it'll give us a chance to catch up." "That's because we aren't supposed to be spending time together" I tell him sarcastically.

Once I get settled, we make ourselves comfortable in the living room. I avoid sitting on the couch with him and opt for sitting at the bar instead. "Do you mind if I order us pizza for dinner? I haven't had time to go get groceries lately." "That's fine. I can pay half" I tell him. "No it's okay. I got it" Jake replies. Jake orders the pizza and then we both resume sitting in our awkward silence. It's not that I don't know what to talk about it. I'm just not sure what I can talk about without bringing up our past. "I might go ahead and take a shower while we wait" Jake says as he rises up from the couch. "Alright" I say as I watch him go into his room and shut the door.

Great, I'm not sure what's worse, sitting here trying to figure out what to talk about or sitting here alone with nothing to do. I wish I would've left my back pack out here so I could study. I decide I'll just check my social media, but as I pat myself down I realize I left my phone in the room too. Just lovely, I think to myself. Maybe I can sneak in and grab my phone real quick. When I hear the shower start, I wait a minute before I approach the door. I slowly turn the knob and to my luck it's unlocked, I open the door and I can see my phone on the night stand. I tip-toe over to the stand and swiftly grab my phone and turn to make my escape, but I am thrown off guard by Jake's naked presence. Jake quickly snatches his towel off the bed and wraps it around him as I turn back to face the wall. "What are you doing?" I ask frantically. "Me? What are you doing?" "I just came to grab my phone. Geez, I didn't know you were going to be standing around butt naked" I say. "Well I forgot my towel" he says. "Sorry" I mutter as I make escape while keeping my eyes on the ground. I feel mortified. I've only been here an hour and things are already a circus.

Just as Jake remerges from his room, the doorbell rings and indicates that the pizza is here. I think we both know better than to draw attention to the shower fiasco so we just take our pizza and retreat to our seats. Jake turns on the TV and scrolls through the channels and settles on a movie that happens to be one of the first movies we saw together. I wonder if he's even aware. Shortly after the movie ends I pick up my mess and tell him that I am going to bed. It's not that I don't want to spend time with him, it's just hard being around him when I can't be myself around him anymore. It also doesn't make sense to deepen the connection we share when I am leaving in a couple weeks.

The next morning, I wake up feeling well rested. I stretch and get out of bed. It's only ten in the morning, but I feel like I have slept for two days. I think my body is finally starting to recover some. After I get ready for the day, I make my way into the living room and I can see Jake putting away groceries. "You went to the store?" I ask surprised. "Yeah. Did you just get up?" He asks me. "Yeah. Wow, I can't believe I didn't hear you leave" I tell him. "You must have been out of it" he replies. "I guess so" I say. I start helping him put away the groceries when I come across a bottle of wine. "Who's the wine for?" I ask him. "It's for you. I remembered that it's your favorite." So he has been recalling some things. I am just about to ask him the extent of what he has remembered when my phone erupts with a loud ring. I pull out my phone but I don't recognize the number, it's a local number though.

"Hello" I say softly. "Hi, Ms. Caldwell this is Natalie with the Family Practice Clinic. I was just wanting to confirm that you'll be able to make it to your follow up appointment today at three." Shoot, I totally forgot about that, I think to myself. "Um, yes. I will be there" I tell the lady. "Great see you then" she says and then hangs up.

"Who was that?" Jake asks. "Just a lady from the clinic I went to. She wanted me to follow up after I had time to process everything and see how I was doing." "And how are you doing?" Jake asks me. "I mean, I still feel shocked at the thought I had baby inside me, but they said I wasn't far along when it happened so I feel a sense of relief. I think at the time, I was being so reckless with my life that it wouldn't have been a good outcome for the baby anyway." My eyes start to water and I feel embarrassed that I ever acted such a way. Jake steps close to me and takes my hands in his. "It's not your fault. You didn't know. I'm sure if you would've known, you would have immediately turned your life around. If anything I can't help but feel responsible since I was the one that was driving us out there" Jake says and I can see the twinge of pain across his face. "Are you kidding me?" I tell him. "The whole accident was my fault. You were supposed to pick me up from my parents at seven but I let myself get caught up at the stupid party at Emma's house and I got so wasted. I missed like five of your calls and when you showed up to Emma's it was eight and we were an hour late for the reservations you made. If I would have just not been an idiot, then we wouldn't have had to rush and could have avoided the accident overall" I tell him, giving him a look of regret. "It's not all your fault though. We both share some of the blame and we could spend hours going over what ifs, but unfortunately it happened and now we just have to try our best to cope with it" Jake tells me. "Yeah I know" I tell him. "So when is your appointment?" He asks me. "It's at three." "Would you like me to come with you?" I hesitate to think it over for a moment, but then decide against him coming in hopes of keeping our romantic life at bay. "No, I really need this time to myself. Thank you though" I tell him. "Alright."

I'm not sure if I upset Jake or not because shortly after we put away the groceries he leaves without a word and I am by myself again. When it is time for me to leave for my appointment he is still gone. As I'm driving to the clinic, I think about how this news could be just as upsetting to Jake and I never thought about how it effects him emotionally. He probably wants to talk about how it makes him feel and the guilt starts to hit me. I try to call him to see if he would like to meet me at the clinic but it goes to voicemail. He must really be mad at me. I didn't mean to upset him.

After an hour long appointment, discussing how last weeks sudden revelation made me feel and explaining everything else that has been going on in my life, Dr. Hampton suggests exactly what I have been planning. She tells me the best thing to do is get out of here and start fresh. I tell her I already plan on doing so once I graduate and she is relieved. I admire the fact that she is taking me seriously and didn't suggest some mental health rehab, which is code for some time in the looney bin. That was Dr. Louchski's favorite solution it seemed like. I was so afraid of telling her everything because it all sounds so made up. Hell, I think I even sound crazy sometimes. She gives me a name of another psychiatrist to see as she doesn't seem to be big fan of how Dr. Loucheski has handled things thus far. When we are finished, I thank her for her time and leave. I make my journey back to Jake's place. I am eager to get back so I can apologize for being selfish. Dr. Hampton told me that men can be emotionally distraught about it too so it is important to include both partners in the healing process.

Chapter 19

Thanks to the rush hour traffic I make it back to Jake's a little after five. When I enter the apartment a delicious aroma has my mouth watering and as I take a look around the lights are off but there are a few lit candles scattered around that provide a romantic atmosphere. I suddenly become nervous that Stacy may be here and turn to leave. "Wait" I hear Jake say. I turn back around and see Jake emerge from his room. "What's going on, is Stacy here?" I whisper. "What? No, this is for us" he states. I take a nervous gulp. He walks towards me, "Give me a chance to properly make it up to for not being there for you." "It wasn't your fault. You didn't even know who you were" I tell Jake. "Please, just let me do this for you" he says as he pulls out the chair to his small two person table. I take a seat and watch him walk into the kitchen. He makes both of us a plate and returns to the table. He places a plate in front of me to reveal spaghetti with meatballs and garlic bread on the side. "Would you like some wine with it?" Jake asks. I nod my head and he pours some wine in the glass sitting in front of me and pours himself some as well. I take my first bite and it is delicious. I haven't had spaghetti in so long even though it's one of my favorite meals. Surely this isn't a coincidence? First the wine and now the spaghetti too. "This is delicious" I tell him. "Thank you, I'm glad you like it." "How did you know I like spaghetti?" I ask him. He hesitates for a moment and then looks me in the eyes. "Because I remember" he says in almost a whisper, "the therapy sessions are helping, it's all starting to come back to me" he tells me. I am not sure what to say. This is what I wanted at first, but if his memories and feelings are coming back, then it's going to make things harder on him. "Oh, well that's good" I tell him. "That's it? I thought you'd be a little more excited than that" Jake says with hurt in his tone. "I am. I'm glad you are getting your memories back. I'm just imagining how hard it must be to remember everything now that things are the way they are." He sets down his fork and stares at me intently, "I would rather be tormented with the memories of what it was like to love you. At least then I'll be able to live my life knowing at one point I was yours and you were mine."

His words overtake me and corrupt all my intentions of being good and he knows it. I stand up from my chair quickly and he mimics me. He comes over to me and pulls my body to his. We look into each others eyes for a brief second and then Jake's lips collide with mine. He lifts me up so I wrap my legs around him and he carries me to the couch. He hovers over me as he takes his shirt off and I rub my hands up and down his chest. I lean up to give him another kiss as I let him take off my shirt. When I fall back onto the couch, Jake uses his lips to caress my breasts. A sudden knock at the door startles us both as we look at one another in fright.

We scramble to get up and I gather our clothes as Jake rushes to the door and checks the peephole. "It's Stacy" he mouths. I quickly blow out the candles and I hide my plate and glass of wine. I take the candles and clothes and run to Jake's room and hide in the closet. Just before Jake opens the door, Stacy serves another knock.

"Stacy what are you doing here?" Jake asks. "I just wanted to come by and tell you some exciting news" she says cheerfully. "What's that?" Jake tells her. I put my ear to the door, so I can be sure to hear the news that just couldn't wait. "Tuesday is our next appointment and we will get to find out if the little bean is a boy or a girl" Stacy says as she lets out an excited squeal. Jake is silent

148

for a moment, "Wow, um that's exciting" he says. "I cannot wait. What do you hope it is?" She asks him. "I don't care as long as it's healthy" Jake says. "Oh come on. You must have a preference?" "Well, if you would have asked me a couple weeks ago I probably would have said a boy, but now I am leaning towards a girl because I would like to name her Elizabeth" Jake tells her. His statement shocks me. My middle name is Elizabeth and I'm sure that isn't a coincidence either. "Hmm, I think we could work with that, but what if it's a boy? What would you want to name it?" She asks. "How about JJ Junior?" Jake says. "JJ Junior?" She questions. "Yeah short for Jake-Jason Junior" he says as he lets out a chuckle. "Not funny. I'm being serious" Stacy whines. "Well, I don't know. Nick, David, Zach? I mean what do you like? I thought the girl picked the names anyway. The guy doesn't usually have a say" he tells her and I can tell he sounds a little frustrated. "Fine. If it's a girl then will name her Elizabeth, but if it's a boy then I'll name him" she says. "Deal" Jake says. I can hear Stacy clearer which means she must be closer to the bedroom. "You up for some company? I can stay the night and we can have some fun?" She says seductively. Yuck, I think I am going to be sick. "I'm pretty tired, I worked today and I was actually taking a nap before you got here." "Oh, well, we don't have to do anything. Just thought it would be nice for us to spend some time together. We can just relax and watch some TV?" She pleads. "Ehh, I don't know Stacy.

I'm just not feeling up for it." "Fine. I'll just go then" she snaps. "Stacy, come on, don't be that way." "How else am I supposed to be? You don't want to touch me, you hardly don't even want to look at me or talk to me. You are the father of our child and you better start acting like it. Sorry I am not good enough, like your precious Sarah, but you were the one who agreed to be with me." "You blackmailed me Stacy. You told me, you wouldn't let me see my child. I am trying here. My life has been one hell of a whirlwind lately and you don't even care how it's effecting me. I'm still figuring out who I am and your worried about how I'm not sleeping with you. Maybe if you would let me have the closure I need then I can process everything better." "Oh, I get it. So what you're saying is you want me to let you run back to Sarah so you two can guilt trip me for not letting you two be together. Excuse me for not wanting our child to be raised in a broken home, like I was. I get that you care about Sarah, but that's why I am trying to help her get my dad locked up. That way you're not always worrying about her and you can focus on us." "What do you mean?" Jake asks confused. "I didn't want to tell you, so that way you wouldn't have to lie if the police started asking questions, but, after you told me about the first set of flowers, it got me thinking. If we could get evidence of my dad threatening her then it would only strengthen her case against him. So, I left the second set of flowers with the threat in hopes that she would report it and help build her case and it worked." I can't believe what I am hearing. It doesn't surprise me that she would do such a thing. I get why she did it and didn't say anything, but to make me suffer through the emotional torment like that is still cruel. "Stacy that is wrong on so many levels. One, you sent Sarah into a panic attack over that and two that's interfering with a case." "You should be thanking me. I did us all a favor. Now my dad is for sure getting locked up and you don't have to obsess over if Sarah is going to be okay each day. Let not forget that my dad can't bully me and my mom anymore. It's a win for everyone, as long as you don't say anything. That is unless, you want Sarah living in fear every time she looks over her shoulder?" Jake is silent. "That's what I thought" Stacy says before continuing "any who, the mood is kind of ruined anyways, so I'll just be going" she says.

I hear the door shut and then I hear Jake lock the bolt on the door, indicating that it's safe for me to come out. Jake approaches me in his room and tries to hug me, but I block him from doing so. "What's wrong?" Jake asks. "What's wrong? Are you serious? We just got cock-blocked by your fiancé who also happens to be the mother of your child. I am not gong to sit here and pretend like I am okay with being a home-wrecker. I love you Jake, but we can't keep doing this to ourselves. It's not healthy for us or the ones around us. You need to focus on your family and I need to focus on myself." Jake's eyes start to well up and his voice cracks when he speaks, "Sarah please." "You think just because you make me dinner and plan a romantic night together that reality isn't going to catch up to us eventually? You're wrong. It's time for us to move on and cut ties" I say as I grab my bags and exit his room. "Where are you going?" Jake asks frantically. "Well it's clear I don't have anything to worry about since it was just Stacy incriminating her father's so I am going back to my grandparents." "Please just stay. We can talk this over" Jake pleads. "It's too late Jake" I say as I walk out the door. I feel the tears fall from my eyes, but I don't turn around, I keep walking to my car.

Although Jake would disagree, what I just did hurt me probably as much as it hurt him. That's what they call tough love and man is it tough. I feel like such an asshole, but it had to be done. We can't keep playing this cat and mouse game. I mean when would it end? The sad truth is, if I let it, we would probably still be pining after one another even after they get married. I have to face facts once and for all, Jake isn't mine anymore. That's why when I make it back to my grandparents I submit every application I can to my dream job listings in Atlanta. I spend the next few hours researching apartments and the surrounding area. By time I go to sleep I am feeling hopeful in the outlook of my future.

Chapter 20

Before I know it, the weekend flies by and I have done a good job of alienating myself from Jake. I haven't answered any of his calls or texts, but now that Monday is here and I have to face Jerry in court later this morning, all I want is to hear his voice so he can tell me everything will be okay. I haven't told Thomas what I found out while I was at Jake's because that means I would have to tell him the whole story. Besides the less people that know, the better. Heck I'm not even supposed to know, so it's not even my secret to tell.

Thomas rolls over and looks up at me with a scowl. "What?" I ask him. "You hardly slept, didn't you?" "Eh, I'll be okay. I'll be able to sleep as much as I want after today" I tell him. "Fair enough" he tells me as he gives me a kiss on the forehead before getting out of bed. "Want me to make you some breakfast?" Thomas asks me. "I'm too nervous to eat anything, but help yourself" I reply. "No that's alright. I just want to make sure you are taken care of."

As I get ready, I intentionally don't put any makeup on so the jury can see my now greenish yellow black eye that Jerry gave me. After all, it is part of the evidence. It's only fair they get to see what he did to me. I finish getting ready and head downstairs. My grandparents meet us at the foot of the stairs. My grandpa gives me a warm smile and opens his arms for a hug. I walk over to him and let him embrace me and it helps fuel me with the strength to go on. "Ready to get this over with?" My grandma asks. "Most definitely" I tell her.

As soon as we walk out of the house, Hector pulls up with the limo and we load up. The ride to the courthouse is quiet, but I hardly notice as my nerves are all over the place. I take one of my Valium before we pull up, that way I don't give Jerry the satisfaction of seeing how he gets to me. None of them say anything as I toss back the pill and take a swig of water. When we arrive we all check through security and file into the room. As I sit there waiting for everyone else to show up, the room feels cold and eery, but as more and more people show up, it starts to feel stuffy and makes me feel claustrophobic. I turn around and grab a hold of Thomas's hand and he squeezes it while giving me an encouraging smile. I can do this, I tell myself. Be strong. Just as I'm giving myself a pep talk, I spot Jake and Stacy walking in. Jake and I make eye contact for split second before he quickly looks away and guides Stacy to their seat. Not long after they make their entrance, Laura, Stacy's mom shows up. She spots me and I start to sweat as she makes her way over to me. I'm not sure how she is taking this whole situation, will she be relieved or is she going to be upset if he gets convicted? He is the father of her child, but from what I've gathered he hasn't been the most pleasant guy regardless.

"Sarah, how are you feeling?" Laura asks me. "I am doing alright. How, are you?" I say while avoiding eye contact. She places her hand on my shoulder, "Sweetie I am doing fine. I just wanted to come over and say I am so sorry for what happened, but I am glad he is finally paying for his actions. You are so brave to go through with this. If you need anything or anyone to talk to just give me a call" she says as she hands me a business card. "Thank you" I tell her and she nods and walks to her seat next to Stacy and Jake. From what I can see Stacy gives her mom a flustered look, I'm sure it's from associating with the enemy.

When the judge enters we all rise and then take our seats. The officers then bring in Jerry and I can feel myself hold my breathe until he takes his seat. He looks even more sinister than I remember. He has grown out his hair and his face is taken over by a scraggly unkept goatee. When he looks at me I get the shivers and become nauseous. I turn around to see my grandparents and Thomas and they each give me an uplifting smile. Just breathe, you can do this, I tell myself.

The next few hours, consist of me, Jerry, Jake, Stacy, Laura, and Beth each going to the podium and providing our accounts of what happened. I can't help but become emotional as I'm telling my side of the story. I explain how he was treating Stacy and Laura during the party and that he was frustrated that I kept intervening. Then I offer a recount of the assault and how he was wearing a mask and I couldn't tell who it was till he threatened me right before I blacked out. Of course, Jerry's lawyer argued that since my assailant was wearing a mask then there was no way to identify truly who assaulted me and at a time of crisis our minds can trick us into believing what we want to believe. Beth offered much help into providing evidence for the case. She looked at the security cameras for the shop and time stamped when Jerry left the shop and then the officers reviewed the footage at the traffic lights near the pier and was able to identify Jerry's car. Jerry had not left right away, it showed his car leaving a couple minutes prior to Stacy and Jake finding me and calling for help. At the conclusion of the trial, Jerry ends up being charged with a felony of aggravated assault and battery and is convicted to three years in prison with no probation and a fine of five thousand dollars.

I become overwhelmed with emotions and relief and start to cry. I can't believe it's finally over. "You bitch" Jerry shouts. His outburst startles me and I flinch as he tries to come at me. The guards quickly grab him and hold him back. He lets out an evil laugh, "You'll always be weak and worthless" he says. Jake stands up and I can see the rage in his face as he tries to hold back his own outburst. "Get this atrocity out of my courtroom" the judge demands. As they practically carry Jerry out of the room I really let the tears fall now.

I feel two arms wrap around me and I turn to face Thomas as he hugs me tighter. "It's all over now. You don't have anything to worry about" Thomas tells me reassuringly. "I know. I just feel so many things right now" I tell him. My grandparents come and give me a hug and suggest we head back home, I quickly agree as they usher me out to the limo. I can't believe he would do such a thing that would only prove his guilt. I settle with the thought that Jerry is just malicious to the core.

Oddly enough, the next two weeks fly by. It's now finals week and everyone is stressing. I do not feel entirely confident, given all my previous distractions, but I can still pass my classes with the grades I currently hold. After court, I isolated myself from everyone. Although it is a relief to know Jerry is locked up, it only served as motivation to focus on myself and do my best to get the hell out of this place. I still haven't talked to Jake, he tried to contact me after court, but I stayed true to my word. Thomas has had quite a few away games so I haven't even spent much time with him either. I'm not complaining it has given me time to catch up on some well needed studying. I even joined a last minute study group, which is what I am currently wasting my time doing. They aren't really discussing anything productive and each of them have calculated their grades to see the lowest grade they can make to pass the class. Which I did submit to peer pressure and do as well, but hey it's good information to know. If only calculating the data and problems on the final would be that easy. I decide to leave the group with the excuse that I need to go study for my final that is tomorrow. Which isn't necessarily a lie, my first final is tomorrow. However, out of all my finals, tomorrows is the one I'm least worried about.

I end up meeting with Thomas for some lunch and we go to the library to study. I can tell he is hiding it, but he is stressed about his exams. I heard him talking with one of his buddies the other day and if he doesn't do decent on the final, he may not pass the class. The added pressure of me moving away isn't helping the fact, because he's already asked me if I'd still want to be with him if he isn't able to move down till next fall. Which in honesty is fine with me, I need to experience time on my own. I know Thomas is eager to move in together, but I think a year on my own will be the perfect amount of time for me to filter through my feelings and thoughts. Especially without Jake holding me back.

Chapter 21

Finals week goes by in a blur, which I am grateful for. I am ready to catch up on some sleep. I am starting to feel discouraged though when Friday rolls around and I still don't have a solid plan. I've been talking about this elaborate plant to move away once I graduate and now that the time is here, I have no clue what to do. I plop down on my bed and let out a large huff. So much for that, I guess. My phone makes a dinging noise and I pull it up to my face. It's just an email, I think to myself as I toss my phone aside. Wait, I haven't checked my email since I sent out all those applications. I grab my phone and pull up my inbox.

I can't believe I didn't even think to check my email this whole time. I have a response from nearly every place I submitted an application to. Of course some of them said no thanks they're looking for someone with more experience, but I have about four companies who are interested in continuing the interview process. I email each of them back. I guess things are starting to look up after all. I change my notifications to alarm me each time I get an email and then make my way downstairs.

"Well someone seems chipper this morning" my grandma states with a smile on her face. "That's because, as of this morning, she is officially a graduate with her very own Associate's degree" my grandpa chimes in. "Not only that, but, I just replied to four potential employers in Atlanta" I say proudly. "Oh my goodness! Sarah that is wonderful!" My grandma exclaims as she showers me with kisses on each cheek and finishes with a hug. My grandpa lets out a chuckle at the sight of her smothering me. "So what's the plan?" My grandpa asks. "Well I probably won't plan on moving out there until anything is official, but I will have to make a trip out there for the interviews most likely." "That's not necessarily the case. A lot of business will suffice with a tele-interview or a phone interview, especially if they know you are living in another state at the moment. You might give it a try" my grandma suggests. "Good point. If they contact me back I will try suggesting that" I tell them. "Have you told your parents?" My grandpa asks. I let the guilt consume me, I haven't really told them much of anything since me and Jake split up. "Um, no. I haven't" I reply. "Well it's probably better to discuss it in person anyway." "True" I tell him.

Although, they don't host an official commencement ceremony like they do each spring, the school provides a small ceremony for those who graduate in the winter. I wasn't going to participate since I should've already graduated by now, besides it's not like we get to walk across a stage or anything. However, once my grandparents found out, they insisted that it's still a big accomplishment to attain a degree and that it's something that would make my parents proud to see. How could I say no? Which is why today I am tasked with going out and finding a nice outfit to wear for the ceremony. My grandparents try to give me more money to cover the cost for the outfit but I refuse to take their money. They already gifted me a hefty amount of money as my graduation present.

My parents and Haley will be coming in Sunday night and I hope it goes relatively well. I'm sure my grandparents have kept them updated on my crazy life since me and Jake have been back. Normally they pester me with calls and texts, but this time around I think they knew better than to poke and prod. I'm curious if Jake will be at the ceremony and I already know if he is, then that means Mary will be there too...and most likely Stacy. As the thought crosses my mind, I begin to have second thoughts on participating, but I can't let them control my happiness anymore. I'll have my own support system there.

As I am out trying on outfits, I get a phone call from an unknown number. "Hello" I say. "Hi, this is Juan with Dreams to Reality Incorporate. I was looking for a miss Sarah Caldwell." I have a silent freak out session. This is the company that I am most interested in. "Yes, this is her" I try to say without my voice cracking. "Great. We received your resume and application and just saw that you gave your notification of graduation." "Yes, that is correct. I can provide an official transcript once the grades are recorded." "That would be excellent. I was wondering if now would be a good time to conduct a phone interview?" I look around the walls of the dressing room as I think to myself how this isn't the most ideal location, but I didn't want to have to reschedule. "Absolutely" I say enthusiastically.

The next thirty minutes are terrifying but oddly satisfying. He asks me questions about what kind of work ethic I think I have and what skills I can offer versus another candidate. He also asks if I will be comfortable with relocating to Atlanta upon a job offer. He asks a few more questions but finishes by asking when the soonest I'd be able to start is and I tell him by the end of the month, contingent upon the offer that is. He sounded pleased with all my answers, but that doesn't mean they are going to pick me I tell myself. He tells me that he has a couple other calls to make, but they will let me know by Monday what the verdict is. By time I get off the phone I feel like I am going to barf. It's hard for me to focus on finding an outfit after that so I just put everything up and make my way back home. Maybe I'll try again tomorrow.

Saturday I mange to occupy my time with Thomas. He takes me out to celebrate my graduation and ends up staying the night. It's not till Sunday evening when my parents and Haley arrive that I feel like I'm going to explode with anticipation. For the most part everyone is on good terms and in a cheerful mood. No one brings up everything that has happened between my last visit home and now and I am relieved. I was anticipating my mom ruining the positive vibe with her nagging questions. I'm sure they will come, but for now, she is letting us relish in the good times.

The next morning I am woken up by a faint ringing. I feel for my phone and retrieve it from under my pillow and blink until I can see the number clearly. "Oh shit" I say. I quickly answer the phone, "Hello, this is Sarah speaking" I say hoping to hide the sleepiness in my voice. "Hi Sarah, this is Juan again. How are you?" "I'm swell, how are you?" Swell? Why on earth did I say that. "Well, I think you are about to be doing much better than swell. I am calling to extend a job offer with Dreams to Reality

Inc. for the Executive Assistant position." "Seriously?" I say excitedly and then clear my throat, "I mean that's great news" I tell him. He lets out a chuckle, "It's okay to be excited, but yes seriously. You will be a full time employee so I will email you the list of benefits. In regards to pay, you will start out at eighteen dollars an hour and will be eligible for annual raises along with raises based on performance. If you accept the offer I'll need you to electronically sign the contract that I'll be sending to your email and then send it back." "I will get that done as soon as I receive it" I tell Juan. "Great, I'll be on the lookout for the document. Do you have any questions for me?" "Not at this time" I tell him. "Alright, well if you have any questions feel free to give us a call. Also, be on the lookout for any further details we will be sending you. Including your schedule that we will start working on." "Sounds great, thank you" "My pleasure and welcome aboard Sarah! Can't wait to meet you in person" Juan says and then hangs up. Once I'm sure the call is over I let out an excited squeal. I jump out of bed and do a happy dance and then make my way downstairs to greet my family.

"Gooood morning" I sing as I round the corner. "Well good morning sweet pea" my grandpa says. "Where is everyone?" I ask. "Looks like we are the only early birds today" he jokes. I give him a playful frown and cross my arms. "Well spill it" he says giving me a grin. "I got the job offer" I tell him. "Oh sweet pea, that is wonderful

news. I'm so happy for you" he tells me. "Thank you" I
tell him with a beaming smile, "I can't wait to tell
everyone else" I say. "They are going to be so excited.
Have you looked at places yet?" He asks me. "I've looked
at a couple, but it's never the same as seeing it in person.
I'm making a list of ones to check out once I get there
though." "That's smart. When do you think you'll leave?"
"Well I told him I could start by the end of the month, so,
I'll probably have to leave sometime next week. That way
I have time to get settled and get familiar with the area."
"Good thinking. It sounds like you have a better handle
on it than you thought" he tells me.

It's not long before everyone else wakes up and
gathers in the kitchen for breakfast. I reveal my good
news and they are all excited and suggests going out for
lunch to celebrate. After lunch me and Haley break off on
our own to go do some shopping. I still haven't found an
outfit for tomorrow, but Haley can help with that.

I should've known it wouldn't be long before they
started asking questions. Once we get to the mall, Haley
starts her not so subtle interrogation. "So how have things
been?" Haley asks. "They've been alright" I reply.
"Grandma told us about that sick freak Jerry. I'm glad
you're okay" she tells me. "Yeah. I guess I got pretty
lucky" I tell her. "What do you think about this outfit?" I
ask, trying to change the subject. "Eh, that's too bland.
What about something like this?" She says as she holds
up a cocktail dress. "Um, no way. That's too revealing" I

reply. "Oh come on. You afraid oh what's his name will get jealous?" She says lightly. I give her a sharp look, "No. Thomas wouldn't mind" I say trying to make it clear that I'm not concerned with Jake. "So, you two are still going strong I take it?" "Yes, we are doing good thanks for asking" I say trying to cut her off. She grabs me by the elbow and I turn around to face her. "Sarah, I'm just worried about you. You've had a bunch of shitty things happen to you. Let me be the over protective big sister." "Look, yes, me and Jake called it quits. He has a baby on the way with a girl who happens to be the devil reincarnated and her dad who almost beat me to death, forced him to propose to her. Does that mean that I can't persevere from it all? No. I'm content with Thomas, he is sweet and caring and treats me well. I just landed an awesome job in Atlanta that, although I might be slightly nervous, I am still very excited to start fresh in a new place. So excuse me for not wanting to focus on the past." "Alright, alright, got it" she says. "I'm not trying to be mean. I'm happy you're here and I'm enjoying our time together. I just want you to be happy for me" I tell her. She loops her arm around mine, "I am happy for you. I just want to make sure that you truly are happy and not just settling." I give her a reassuring smile and we continue our journey of finding the right outfit, but the truth is I'm just putting on big facade. The harder I try to forget Jake, the more my heart longs for him.

The next morning, the house is buzzing with life as everyone is getting ready for the ceremony. For the first time in a long time we actually feel like a family. As I look back over the last six months it's surreal how much my life has changed. I can't help but feel proud over how much I was able to overcome. I'm not going to lie, I had my moments of doubt, but I stuck through it and now I finally get to graduate and start my own life. When we all finish getting ready, they take turns taking pictures with me. It makes me feel proud. "Alright, everybody, it's time to load up or we're going to be late" my dad says.

We make it to the college just in time for me to check in and find my place for the seating arrangement. Luckily there's not much time before the ceremony, because Jake is here and so is his anti-Sarah club. The speaker announces for us to take our seats and shortly after starts the ceremony. The speaker who turns out to be the vice president of the facility delivers his speech over "continuing to strive for excellence" and offers his words of encouragement and wisdom. He then proceeds to announce each persons name and the degree they attained. The only difference is we don't get to get up and walk across a stage and get handed a fake diploma. When he finishes announcing our names, we all rise and let the people applaud us for a moment and then we are dismissed to the lobby for refreshments.

Once my family makes their way over to me, they all gather around and congratulate me once more. It's not long before Thomas and his parents approach us. I can see the unsettling look on my moms face when I introduce Thomas to her and the rest of the family. I already know what she's thinking, but I don't care. "Teresa, Dwayne, thank you for coming" I tell them. "Of course, congratulations kiddo" Dwayne says and gives me a pat on the back. Teresa is her typical self and opts for a hug though. They then introduce themselves to my parents and Haley. This whole situation is awkward. "These are for you" Thomas says as he hands me a bouquet of flowers. "You're so sweet, thank you" I tell Thomas. "Look at the card" he says with a mischievous grin. I open the card and it reads *Love your not so secret admirer.* I laugh which prompts him to laugh. "Well aren't you funny" I tell him. "Maybe just a little" he says as he takes a step closer to me. Our faces are inches apart when we hear an "Ahem" come from behind us. At first I thought it was my dad, but to my surprise it's Jake.

"Jake, hi" I say as I take step back. "I just wanted to say congrats. I know you are going to do great things" Jake tells me. "Hell yeah she is. She is going to kill it out in Atlanta" Thomas states. I look at Thomas horrified that he just let my personal secret slip. I look at Jake and he looks as if someone just sucker punched him in the stomach. "Wait, what?" Jake says confused. "Thomas can you give us a minute" I say to him. He gives me a remorseful nod at the realization of what he just did.

"What is he talking about?" Jake asks flabbergasted. "I'm moving" I say throwing up my hands in defeat. "To Atlanta?" He says rhetorically. "When were you going to tell me?" He asks devastatingly. "I wasn't" I say in a near whisper. He gives me a heart shattering look and I can't stand the sight of seeing him hurt so I turn to make my escape. He grabs my hand and I look back at him once more. "But I love you" he says as he lets the tears fall. "Well don't" I say as I snatch my hand back and make a beeline for the bathroom. I tell myself not to turn back when I hear his heart wrenching sob as I walk away. I make it to the bathroom and splash my face with some cool water. I text Haley and tell her that I'm ready to go, this whole ordeal is too much for me. Luckily I can always count on Haley. Within minutes of texting her she already has an extraction plan devised. She comes to bathroom and guides me out the building to where my parents and grandparents are already waiting in the limo.

Chapter 22

It's finally moving day and I have my few belongings loaded up and ready to head to Atlanta. Since it's officially winter break, Thomas is tagging along and will help me with the apartment hunting process. Also, there's no way I can make that drive on my own, so, he is going to help drive and then catch a flight back. Before leaving I give my grandparents an extra long hug and thank them for everything.

"Call us if you need anything" my grandmas says. "I sure will" I reply. "Love you sweet pea. You two be safe and let us know when you make it" my grandpa adds. "We will" I tell them. My grandma starts to tear up, "Awe grandma don't cry, you can come visit anytime" I tell her reassuringly. "I may have to take you up on that offer. Do you know how many contracts I get in Atlanta?" She says quickly, resuming her professional demeanor. I let out a chuckle, "I'm sure it's a bunch" I say. "Alright dear, we need to let them get on the road. There's only so much daylight" my grandpa says as he pries my grandma off of me. "Thomas, take care of our girl" my grandpa says sternly, yet compassionately. "Of course, sir" Thomas replies as he offers a handshake to my grandpa. Thomas then kisses my grandmother's hand and we make our escape to the car. My grandparents wave us off until eventually we reach the gate and I can't see them anymore. "Here we go" I say out loud, subtly seeking affirmation. "Here we go" Thomas repeats and flashes me a smile.

It takes us five days to make it all the way to Atlanta. We couldn't have made it at a better time because I don't think I could've handled being in the car for another minute. The trip wasn't so bad though. Thomas and I really had a chance to bond and it gave me a glimpse of what it might be like when he's around all the time.

I should've known not to expect anything less from my grandparents when we pull into the five star hotel that they booked for us. I'm guessing I have a week to find a place because that's how long they have our room booked. Of course it's too late to start apartment hunting today so we will just have to start fresh tomorrow.

The next morning we have three tours scheduled and another two the following day. Since our first tour doesn't start till eleven, we decide to venture around the area and find a tasty looking breakfast joint nearby. As we sit in the restaurant, I can't keep myself from staring out the window. It feels unreal to be here, to actually be doing this.

"Are you excited?" Thomas asks. "Yes" I say giving him a big smile. He returns the smile, "Good. It makes me happy to see you so happy" he replies. "Thank you Thomas, and thank you for supporting me and helping me move out here" I tell him. "Of course. I just want you to be happy" he says. "I am" I tell him. By time we finish eating, it's time for us to head to the first apartment complex.

I guess I did not realize how expensive it will be to live out here, because it seems that the average monthly rent is $1,300 for a decent place. "I don't think I can afford any of these on my own" I say sadly to Thomas after leaving the second complex. "I'll barely be able to afford rent with one check. I've done the math" I whine. "Maybe they can split up the payment. Half at the beginning of the month and the other half in the middle of the month" Thomas suggests. "It doesn't work that way" I say as I start to get pouty. "Could you ask your grandparents for money to cover you until you get some money saved up?" I give him a frustrated look, "No. I don't want to take anymore of their money. They have already done so much. This is something I need to do on my own" I say. He throws his hand up in the air, "Okay, okay. We will figure it out then" he tells me calmly.

When we finish touring the last complex, I start feeling hopeless. It's not that I don't like the places, because I do. I just don't know how I am going to afford it. On the way back to the hotel we get lost and end up in some town called Tucker. "This town seems nice" Thomas comments. "Yeah, it's pretty quaint" I reply. "It doesn't seem to be that far from Atlanta. You might look at the options around here" Thomas suggests. "Good idea" I say as I pull out my phone and begin to browse the listings for the area. "Wow the more expensive ones seem to be in the lower to mid nine hundred range" I say positively. "That sounds a lot more promising" he tells me. "I really like this one" I say enthusiastically as I swipe through the pictures, "they close at five, that's in thirty minutes" I say. "Well then we better head that way" Thomas says.

Fortunately, the manager is nice enough to give us a last minute tour when we arrive. Even though it was rushed, I really liked the apartment and the vibe I got. So much so, that I submitted an application and she told me she would get back with me in about two days. I paid my application fee and we left. "I really hope this one works out" I tell Thomas. "Me too. That place is pretty cool. I like how open it is." "I know I love the open floor plan" I tell him excitedly. "I almost don't want to see the other ones tomorrow, but I don't want to jinx my luck" I tell him.

The next day we go through with the tours and when we finish we decide to go do some shopping. Even though I don't have a place set in stone yet, I need to have an idea of what furniture I would like to have. Having everything picked out will make the moving in process that much smoother. I let Thomas have some of the say since ultimately he will be living with me. Not going to lie though, I am a bit nervous about Thomas going back to California. I've never done a long distance relationship before and I'm just not sure how it will work out.

It's not till Friday that I get a call from the apartment complex in Tucker informing me that I am approved and can start moving in tomorrow as long as I come get the keys today. I gladly accept and we immediately leave to get the keys. On the way back we make a stop so I can buy a few of the essentials that I'll need. Who knew buying cleaning supplies, a trash can, and a broom would be so exciting? When we make it back to the hotel, I go online and order a bed and some other furniture to be delivered on Monday. Once I get everything settled in my apartment I can then focus on getting orientated at work. I'm sure they will be pleased to know that I can start a few days earlier if needed. As of right now my start date is December 20th. They wanted to get me in before the holidays because it's a high volume time for business, but if I can get everything situated by Monday then I can start a couple days early.

We spend the weekend moving things into the new place and buying stuff for the apartment. I try not to focus so much on the decorating aspect because I can do that over time. Plus, decor is so expensive. Why is everything so expensive? By time Monday rolls around, the furniture I ordered is delivered and serves as the finishing touches. It doesn't look very glamorous, but it looks homey and that's all that matters. As Thomas finishes putting together the TV stand in the living room our pizza is delivered and we can finally sit back and relax.

"Whew. Glad to have that done" Thomas says as he wipes his brow and plops down on the couch. "Thank you so much Thomas. I don't know what I would have done without out you" I tell him. "It's no problem, I'm glad I could help." I hand him his plate of pizza and then make myself cozy next to him. "This is nice" I say proudly as I look around the place. "It sure is. You should be proud" Thomas tells me. "I still can't believe I'm going to be living here by myself" I tell him. "Speaking of" Thomas says and then hesitates before continuing, "now that you're settled, when did you want me to head back?" Thomas asks glumly. I've been so caught up in everything that I didn't even think about Thomas leaving. It's been nice having him around, especially with such a big transition. I'm not sure if I'm ready for him to leave though. "Well...I've been thinking. What if you stayed for another week or so? I know you'll be alone while I'm at work so I understand if you don't want to stick around" I say. "Are you kidding? I'd love too" Thomas says eagerly.

Tuesday we spend the day getting me miscellaneous office supplies that I might need and finding me business casual outfits. Tomorrow is my first day of work and I want to make the best first impression. My anxiety starts to trigger all my negative thoughts. What if I mess up and they start to hate me already? I try to push the negative thoughts out of my head as I focus on deciding which new outfit I should wear for tomorrow.

"Which one do you think?" I ask Thomas as I hold up two outfits to choose from. "Hm, the left one. It really brings out your eyes" he says giving me a wink. I instantly blush, "Good choice" I say as I set it aside. "Now which shoes? And should I wear a watch or does that make me look like a nerd? Maybe just a bracelet instead?" I say with a flustered tone. Thomas stands up and walks over to me and takes the bracelet and watch from me. "Just breathe. They are going to love you regardless" Thomas says and then hands me back the watch. "I think the watch would look better though" he tells me. I give him a smirk and then follow it with a kiss. "Thank you" I tell Thomas. He wraps his arms around me and gives me a long kiss. When he pulls away I look into his eyes and succumb to his seductive gaze. There's no point in holding back any longer, I tell myself. We fall onto the bed and let our bodies reacquaint themselves with one another.

The next morning I actually wake up before my alarm goes off, feeling less tense and so much more at ease. Despite the first day jitters, I'm in a positive mood and ready to conquer the day. As I get out of bed, I smell the aroma of coffee and it puts a smile on my face. Thomas got up early just to make me coffee. I immediately start getting ready and when I'm finished I meet Thomas in the kitchen.

"Good morning" Thomas says as he hands me a cup of coffee to go. "Good morning and thank you for the coffee" I reply. "You're welcome. I was going to make breakfast, but figured you'd be too nervous to eat it anyway" he says. "Well you figured right" I tell him. "You look great" he tells me. "You think so?" I say as I give a twirl. "I know so" he says as he gives me a kiss. I let out a large huff, "Good. I think I am going to go ahead and leave early since I'm not sure how traffic will be" I tell him. "Good point. Well, good luck, even though you don't need it" he says. "Thank you" I reply and then give him a kiss. I grab my bag after making sure everything is in there for the hundredth time and then I head to my first day of work.

By time Friday rolls around, I am already in love with my job. On Monday I get to start directly working with Nicole, the lady that I'll be working as an assistant for. I have my own small office right outside of Nicole's and I also have my own work phone. They told me to keep it on me at all times in case Nicole needs to get ahold of me. I hope she likes me, but I also hope she isn't mean and takes advantage of me. I guess we'll just have to wait and see.

Sunday evening I get my first text on my work phone from Nicole:

Hi Sarah, this is Nicole. If you could pick me up a coffee tomorrow morning, that will be greatly appreciated. There's a coffee shop just around the corner from work. Large medium roast, two pumps vanilla, one pump hazelnut, one scoop of sugar, and a dash of skim milk. Get yourself something too, my treat, thanks - xoxo

Well, she seems nice. However, she also seems like a diva, but I guess most people who have assistants are entitled to being divas. Should I reply, or does that make me seem like a kiss up? I end up replying after I convince myself that I have to at least her know I received the message: *Sure thing! See you in the morning.*

Now I had my first mission, with one goal, don't screw up her order. I make sure to leave extra early so I have plenty of time to find the coffee shop. After circling around the block twice I finally find it and make my way inside to order the coffee. It's so busy and I end up waiting fifteen minutes before I can place the order. I'm glad I left early I think to myself, who knows how long it'll take for them to make it. When I finally make it to the front of the line, I read the barista word for word her order and then I order a regular vanilla coffee. When I complete my order I take a seat and wait for them to call my name.

In the meantime I pull out my work phone and review over Nicole's schedule today. She has her first meeting at nine. I wonder how I am supposed to prepare for her meetings, they didn't go over that with me. Maybe I can just ask her when I get there? I feel a tap on my shoulder and I swivel around in my chair. My jaw drops open when I see who it is.

"Blake? What the heck are you doing here?" I ask astonished. He points to a table in the back, "I was sitting back there writing when I glanced up and saw you sitting here. I didn't believe my eyes at first, but when I got up to get my coffee I saw it was you." I give him a look of suspicion. "I promise. No secrets this time" he tells me. "I just can't believe it. How'd you end up out here?" I ask him. "Well after your stunt in Kentucky, Mary let us go and told us to get out of California and to never contact her again. She compensated us well and I used to the money to come out here in hopes of finally starting my journalism career" he tells me. I nod slowly as I process it all. "What a small world" I tell him. "I know it's crazy. But, how are you? How's Jake?" He asks. I look away, I had done a good job of not thinking about him until now. "Um. I'm good. I'm guessing Jake is doing fine" I tell him. "Wait, I thought you two were together again?" He asks. I let out a sigh, "We were. Until we got back from Kentucky and he found that Stacy was pregnant and she blackmailed him into being with her or she wouldn't let him see the kid. Then on top of that her dad forced him to get engaged to her" I say. "Hold up, hold up. Stacy is pregnant?" Blake asks looking horrified. "Yep" I say. "Are you sure she's actually pregnant?" He asks me. "Jake has gone to some of the appointments with her so it must be legit" I tell him. "Sarah!" I hear the barista shout. "That's mine, I gotta get going. Nice seeing you though" I say to Blake. I quickly make my way over to grab the coffees and then head to work.

Chapter 23

I can't help but feel a little blue as I realize that tomorrow will be New Years day. Which means in four days, Jake will be married to Stacy. It's been a little over a week and a half since I ran into Blake and I've had a hard time of keeping Jake out of my thoughts since then. I wish he would've never seen me, but for some reason fate led us to each other once again for some odd reason. Is it so I have a friend out here in Atlanta?

I try to brush off my thoughts down memory lane as I finish getting ready for tonight. Me and Thomas are going out to celebrate the New Year's Eve festivities. As Thomas gets in the shower, I retreat to the room to put on some makeup. I am just about finished when I hear a knock at the door. I wonder who that could be? I make my way to the door and check the peephole. To my surprise it's Blake.

"What are you doing here? And how did you find out where I live?" I hiss. He won't look me in the eye and rubs his neck nervously, "I promise I'm not stalking you. I just had to talk to you again after I saw you at the coffee shop" he tells me. "Well then you better get to talking before I call the cops" I tell him. "Look, just hear me out. When you told me Stacy was pregnant, I freaked out. I'm not proud to admit it, but me and Stacy hooked up a couple times. She just kept throwing herself at me and I knew it wasn't right, but I was dumb." I hold up my hand to silence him. "I don't need to hear all of your dirty details. Just tell me when you two started hooking up" I say sternly. "I'm not for sure. Sometime mid to late September I think." "Well then you can save your sudden urge for repentance because they slept together the beginning of September" I tell Blake, "now get out of here before Thomas comes out" I say. "No. You don't get it. I did some digging and she would be much further along if Jake got her pregnant. "You don't know what you're talking about" I say frustratingly. "Look!" He says as he pulls out some papers from his bag. I looked into her appointment records, which also happened to be paid for by the almighty Ms. Henson" he says as he points at the record. "That's not all," he says as he shuffles the papers around until he finds the one he's looking for. "This here shows that Mary had the doctor do an undisclosed paternity test when doing an amniocentesis, but it wasn't on the actual bill, which means Mary paid the doctor under the table to do it without letting Stacy know. Which if you notice, the results show there is no match to Jake Mason Henson being the father." I use the wall for support to keep me from passing out. This means, Jake isn't the father and Ms. Henson has been covering it up this whole time. " I would've told you sooner, but I wanted to be sure before I got your hopes up" Blake tells me. "I don't know what to say" I tell him while still in shock. "Come with me" he urges, "I have the proof that the kid is mine and you and Jake can finally be together" Blake says. "How do you know for sure?" I say skeptical of his so called proof. "Glad you asked" he says as he retrieves one last paper. "I called the office and accused them of their shady dealings with Mary Henson and told them that I would keep quiet if they allowed me to submit a sample to test for paternity. I told them not to say a word to Mary or I'd report them. Anyways, I got this in the mail today," Blake says as he hands me the piece of paper. The paper establishes that Blake's DNA is a high genetic match. "I can't believe this" I murmur as I hand him back the paper. "It says it right here" Blake says defensively. "I know that. I just mean that this is just astonishing" I say. "This has to be a sign. What are the odds that we run into each other after all this time, in a completely different state?" He tells me. He has a point, but it doesn't matter. "Well, you're too late. They get married on the fourth" I tell Blake. "Then we better get going" he says frantically. "You don't get it" I say angrily. "It takes five days to drive there and even if I could just up and leave. I don't have the money to buy a plane ticket. Plus I just started my job, they aren't going to just let me take off. That would make me look so bad." I say flustered. "I'm sure they'd understand if you'd explain the situation" Blake says. "No, I'm not going to risk my new job by telling them how much of basket case my life is." "Fine! Don't blame me when you realize that you missed your opportunity to be with Jake once and for all" Blake says and then storms off.

I shut the door and walk over to the couch and plop down. I hear the shower turn off and feel grateful that Thomas didn't hear any of the conversation. I didn't even feel like going out anymore, but I don't want to give off that anything is wrong. I feel bitter and angry, but I have no one to blame but myself. I'm the one giving up when all I ever wanted is now within arms reach. I wipe the tears away and resume my composure before going back in the room.

"You look great" Thomas says as I walk in the door. "Thank you" I say, mustering the best smile I can. I wait for Thomas to finish getting ready and then we make our way downtown. I try my best not to be a buzzkill and enjoy our time together. I originally didn't plan on getting drunk, but when we made it to the club I couldn't help but drown may sorrows in alcohol. Once the alcohol hits my system it helps numb me and I'm able to let loose a little. We dance the rest of the night a way and when midnight hits I'm expecting a big fat kiss from Thomas, but he opts for a kiss on the hand instead. He must really not like the thought of taking advantage of me while I'm drunk. Talk about a keeper.

By Tuesday I think I have finally recovered from my hangover, which is good since I have to go back to work today. Thomas took care of me the whole time and it reassures me that I am making the right decision to stay where I'm at. I get up and get ready for work and plan on stopping to get coffee. This time my treat because I'll need it to keep my headache at bay. As I get ready to leave I panic because I can't find my work phone. Thomas finds it for me and it makes me wonder what I'm going to do when he leaves this weekend.

When I make it into work I give Nicole her coffee and then take my place at my desk. I try my best to focus on work, but it's a losing battle. The thought of Jake getting married in practically a day and a half has me struggling mentally. That's why when Nicole calls me into her office, I'm sure it's because I've done something to mess up.

"Sarah, please come in and have a seat" Nicole tells me. "Is there something I can do for you?" I ask her nervously. "Actually there is" she says. "Alright" I say as I pull out my pen, ready to take notes. "There's a location we are thinking about merging with and we need a couple people from each department to go to the location for a photoshoot they are hosting" she tells me. I give her a blank stare. "I was hoping you could go and represent us" she tells me with a smile. "Really? It would be an honor" I tell her. "Good. You'll need to start packing because you leave tomorrow. "Wait. Where is it?" I ask. "It's in California. Which works out great, aren't you from there?" She asks. "Technically," I tell her, still a little shocked. There's no way this is real, I think to myself. It can't be a coincidence that I am going to California the day before Jake gets married. "Great. Then you need to go meet with Shatasha from the makeup department and Rachel with hair so you all can collaborate" Nicole says. I give her a nod to show that I understand. "So will I just be their assistant for the trip?" I ask. She lets out a laugh, "No, you are my assistant. I just need you to go in and fill in as the model" she tells me. "A model?" I say shocked. I become uneasy in my seat. I don't have the physique of a model and let's not forget about my scars. "No offense Nicole, but I'm not really the model type" I say. She shakes her head, "Now that's not really the attitude I like to hear. I think every person is capable of being a model. Whose to say what qualities define a model?" She says intently. "In fear of upsetting her further I quickly agree. "You are very right. I'm sorry if I offended you. I just have never modeled before" I tell her. "It's alright, I understand that it seems terrifying, but I'm sure you're going to enjoy it" she tells me. I simply nod, to avoid opening my big mouth once more. "Now go on and meet the other girls. When you are done you can go home early so you can pack. You should be receiving your plane ticket by email" she tells me. "Got it. Thanks again for the opportunity" I tell her and then leave to meet Shatasha and Rachel.

After running through a couple different looks with the girls I head home. I'm not sure how I'm going to break the news to Thomas. Let's not forget about the fact that this has to be a sign that me and Jake are supposed to be together. Now I have to get Blake on board otherwise, I don't have the proof that I need in order to crash the wedding. I try to call Blake, but it goes straight to voicemail. Great, now I'm starting to panic. When I make it to the house, I tell Thomas the news and he doesn't seem to be thrilled, but he also isn't upset about it. Im sure it has to do with the fact that by time I get back from California it'll be time for him to leave and that's got him mellow. How will I break it to Themas though if I go through with my plan to stop Jake's wedding?

When the three of us land in California, we immediately head to our hotel. Shatasha and Rachel are giddy with excitement, they have never been to California before. I wish I could be as excited as them. I still haven't got a call back from Blake and I have left him numerous voicemails. I'm not even sure if it's still his number. Without his proof, I can't accuse Stacy of anything. I'll just look like a psycho ex, that'll end up being dragged out. After much pleading, I end up taking the girls to the pier so I can show them around and fulfill their wanderlust desires. I hate to admit it but I pass by the shop Jake works at in hopes of seeing him, but he's not there. I don't blame him, I probably wouldn't be working the day before my wedding either.

The next morning we get up and head to the venue. From what I can see when we pull up it's a small rustic vineyard. "This place is adorable" Shatasha says. "These photos are going to turn out amazing" Rachel comments as she nudges me. I reply with a nervous laugh. We make our way into the building and are greeted by the photographers, stylist, and the owners of the vineyard. Once we get the formalities out of the way they show us to a room where we can start getting ready. Rachel does my hair first and styles it in a flattering updo. Next, Shatasha does my makeup with an agreed upon neutral look and adds a hint of pink to my lips.

"Beautiful! Now for the finishing touch" Candace, the stylist says as she disappears for a moment before returning with a white bag. She unzips the bag to reveal a wedding dress inside. I can't help myself as I let out gasp. "What's wrong? You don't like it?" Candace asks. "No, not at all. It's beautiful" I tell her reassuringly. The truth is the dress looks identical to the wedding dress I picked out. "I just didn't realize this was a wedding shoot" I say bit somberly. Of all the days for this to happen too. I slip on the dress and look in the mirror. As I admire my appearance I try to refrain from getting emotional as I feel the burning lump in my throat form. "Girl, you better not mess up my make up" Shatasha says which helps break the tension. I laugh as I fan myself, "I'm sorry, I just have a lot on my mind right now" I tell them. "Well just relax, it's time to have fun" Rachel says. "Are you all ready yet?" One of the photographers ask impatiently. "Yes, we're coming right now" Shatasha replies. "Oh my goodness, I almost forgot the flowers" Candace says as she scurries off once more and returns with a giant bouquet of fresh flowers. "Okay, now you're ready" she says as she shoos me off.

As we exit the building I can hear a soft romantic melody playing in the background to help set the atmosphere. The girls help escort me to the center of the vineyard where a gazebo stands with a man inside that I've never seen before. "Are you supposed to be the groom?" I ask the man. He lets out a chuckle, "No, but he is" he says as he nods past me. I turn around and see Jake approaching the gazebo. I feel like I just got the wind kicked out of me.

"What's going on here?" I say surprised. "You're getting married" Shatasha says as her and Rachel giggle and then quickly leave my side. Jake takes his place in front of me and gives me his heart melting smile. Even though I am so confused at what is going on, I can't help but notice how handsome Jake looks in his tux. "What are you doing?" I ask Jake. "Well, I'm trying to marry the girl of my dreams, if that's okay with you?" He tells me. "I'm just so confused. Where's Stacy? I have so much to tell you and you're not going to believe it." He puts his finger to my lips, "Later. Can we please just get married?" He asks. I nod while giving him my biggest smile. He turns to the strange man and gives him a nod. Rachel takes my bouquet from me and Jake takes my hand in his. The strange man delivers the wedding sermon and when it's our time to say I do, I start crying in disbelief that this is really happening. Jake slips the ring he once gave me on my finger, followed by a shiny band. When it's my turn, Shatasha hands me a silver ring to put on Jake. When the man tells Jake to kiss the bride, Jake tilts me back and gives me one long kiss.

At the conclusion of our ceremony I stand there in shock. Jake sticks out his elbow, "Wife" he says indicating for me to loop my arm around his. I do so and he leads me back inside the building were everyone is smiling and clapping. The man comes up to us once more to have us fill out and sign some papers so that way the marriage can be legalized. I am so overwhelmed with emotion and I have so many questions. When the man leaves, I pull Jake back out to the gazebo so we can have some alone time.

"I love you so much" Jake tells me. "I love you too. Are we actually married though?" I ask him, feeling as if everything is too good to be true. "Not officially. We have to wait for our papers and license to be processed" he tells me. I give him a tight hug as I start to cry. "What's wrong?" He asks. "I thought I was going to lose you forever, today" I tell him between sniffles. He hugs me back and caresses my hair. "Till death do us part" he says. I pull away and smile at my husband. "But how?" I ask, still so confused out how this was even possible. He pulls out an envelope from inside his jacket and hands it to me. "I'm going give some time alone to read this" he says and then kisses me on the forehead before disappearing back into the building.

I open the envelope and pull out a nicely typed letter.
Dear Sarah,

Please don't be mad. I know you hate people interfering in your life, but I couldn't just sit by and pretend like I could be okay with keeping you from true happiness. I didn't want to tell you, but I heard everything the night Blake stopped by. I knew you'd be too stubborn to take him up on your offer. You're too good, I knew that from the start. You are always putting others first and that's why I couldn't let you give up your chance of being with Jake once again. There's only so many signs that the universe can give you, that you two are meant to be together. I spent all day putting this crafty plan together. I called Jake the next day to tell him what I heard and contacted Blake for the proof. Since you and Jake attract so many obstacles in your relationship. We decided that it would be best if we eliminated any other chance of you two from being together by having you two meet at the alter. I contacted Nicole and told her that we needed help pulling off a surprise wedding for you without you knowing. If you're reading this, then that means we have successfully pulled off our plan. Congratulations! Please don't feel guilty, I enjoyed our time together more than you'll ever know, but I'd never be able to live with myself, knowing I kept your from being truly happy and have you end up resenting me for it. After all, endless love finds a way.

Love always,
Thomas